TAINTED REASONING

DARK SOVEREIGNTY BOOK TWO

ANNA EDWARDS

Edward and William my love
Visit!

CONTENTS

Foreword	vii
Chapter 1	1
Chapter 2	11
Chapter 3	21
Chapter 4	33
Chapter 5	45
Chapter 6	53
Chapter 7	63
Chapter 8	71
Chapter 9	79
Chapter 10	87
Chapter 11	95
Chapter 12	103
Chapter 13	109
Chapter 14	115
Chapter 15	127
Chapter 16	137
Chapter 17	147
Chapter 18	155
Chapter 19	163
Chapter 20	171
Chapter 21	181
Chapter 22	189
Chapter 23	195
Chapter 24	203
Chapter 25	213
Chapter 26	223
Epilogue	229

Afterword	235
Coming Soon	237
Acknowledgments	239
The Control Series	241
The Glacial Blood	243
About the Author	245
Meet the Author	247

Copyright © 2018 by Anna Edwards

All rights reserved. No part of this publication may be reproduced, distributed or transmitted in any form or by any means, without prior written permission.

www.AuthorAnnaEdwards.com

This is a work of fiction. Names, characters, places, and incidents are a product of the author's imagination. Locales and public names are sometimes used for atmospheric purposes. Any resemblance to actual people, living or dead, or to businesses, companies, events, institutions, or locales is completely coincidental.

Warning: This book contains sexually explicit scenes and adult language and may be considered offensive to some readers. This book is for sale to adults only, as defined by the laws of the country in which you made your purchase.

Disclaimer: Please do not try any sexual practice without the guidance of an experienced practitioner. Neither the publisher nor the author will be responsible for any loss, harm, injury, or death resulting from the use of the information contained in this book.

Cover Design by www.CharityHendry.com

Logo Design by Charity Hendry

Editing by Tracy Roelle

Formatting by Anna Edwards and Charity Hendry

Proofreading by Sheena Taylor

Tainted Reasoning/ Anna Edwards -- 1st ed.

ISBN 978-1729323625

FOREWORD

Please note this is an unconventional dark romance. There will be triggers.

Thank you for understanding. I hope you enjoy reading.

Anna xx

CHAPTER ONE

WILLIAM

I shut my eyes, allowing the stench of his fear, and his desperation for an end to the suffering, to wash over me. I can feel it surround every fiber of my being, and I revel in it. The man my brother, Nicholas, is currently torturing deserves everything that comes to him. He's a devil in the guise of a human being – landed gentry with a façade so convincing nobody knew for years he abused his daughter, Amelia. He raped her, beat her, and forced her to perform acts so degrading that in the end she placed a pistol against her sweet, innocent head and pulled the trigger. My sister-in-law, Victoria, still wakes in the night screaming from the memory.

Nicholas doesn't know I can hear her way up in the attic area of the mansion we reside in. Her sobs are heartbreaking and make the man, whose fingers and toes are currently being removed, one by one, more than deserving of his punishment. Nicholas' hands are covered in blood. I know he doesn't like to do this. He would rather be home with his new wife, but this has to be done. The evil that exists within the society bearing our family name must be destroyed. It must be wiped from the surface of this planet as penance for the tortures inflicted on innocent girls since the society was founded by our four-times-great-grandfather.

"What you did to Amelia was sick. My name will no longer be associated with such crimes. We'll turn the society into one that honors the female of our species. Rejoicing in her beauty and worshiping her like the goddess she is. We'll not harm anyone, nor will we take any more property that's not ours without consent. Your membership is at an end, and that of your heirs unless they accept my authority and sign their agreement to the new charter I've put in place." My brother stands tall in front of Edgar Rushbrooke. His bloody hands now rest, folded across his chest. He wears a tailored suit that fits his body like a glove. It's an odd choice for the work we are doing, but somehow, it provides him with even more power. I'm in jeans and a t-shirt. I've never had the designer wardrobe my brother has. I've not had need of it, having been locked away since I was a toddler by my father, the previous Duke of Oakfield. Jeans are in fact an upgrade from the jogging bottoms I've previously worn. Green, my t-shirt is green. It always has to be. It's my favorite color, after all, and the only one I'll wear over my toned chest. The shade doesn't matter: forest, olive, mint, or even emerald– it just has to be green. I once borrowed one of Nicholas' t-shirts–he does have a few–it was burgundy, and I felt ill at ease all day. It wasn't right, and I was glad to get back to my comfort color the next day. My uniform.

My unruly brown hair is messily styled with my fingers brushed through it being the only nod to tidiness. Nicholas' is combed to perfection–no doubt by his new wife. I'm sure she's also given him a close shave this morning since his jaw is devoid of any hair. Mine is stubbled with two days' growth. I don't like shaving although I know I have to do it, but it feels strange. I can't explain why–it just seems wrong to me. I guess it's because of the autism I suffer from, wiring my brain in such a way that a natural grooming routine feels odd. My brain does that frequently, but thankfully, it also forces me to be a very clean person–I shower several times a day.

The tics start subtly: the swipe of my ear, a tap of my foot, the banging of the fingers of my left hand onto the right. My anxiety of the situation forces me into what I know will become my routine to cope with it.

"William?" Nicholas has turned to face me, and I look up at him. "You ok?"

"Yes," I reply, not wanting to worry him. This is me. The strange movements and oddities are who I am. Not everyone understands it, but I can't change them. They're a fundamental part of who I am and are with me for life.

"Good. Can you pass me the cutters? I want to remove his tongue."

"No!" Edgar shouts out. "Please. It was your father. I didn't want to do anything to Amelia. I loved her. She was my only daughter. The Duke forced me to prepare her. He said he would ostracize me if I didn't, and I couldn't risk that. My title is all our family have left–we've barely got any money left in our estate. I didn't want to do it. I even tried to smuggle Amelia away, but I failed." The once dignified gentleman is now a sniveling wreck. His eyes are blood shot, and snot drips from his nose. It's embarrassing to see how the men of the society respond to some of the tortures, which they would happily inflict on a woman, in other circumstances. Victoria took everything that happened to her with her head held high. This man is a coward, and in a few short moments, he will die like one. I don't hesitate any longer and picking up the cutters, I step forward. Nicholas holds his head straight, and I pull out Edgar's tongue and slice through the muscle. Gargled sounds of pain fill the room, and I shut my eyes, taking them all in. They excite me. The knowledge that this man is suffering gives me great joy. Is that normal?

I throw the bloody tongue onto the fire, which has been lit in the basement, and listen to it crackle as I watch it shrivel up to nothing. It's beautiful. Truthfully, is that reaction normal?

"Brother, the final say is all yours." I walk over to where a comfortable Queen Anne chair is placed in the corner of the room, its leather cover a deep green in shade. Nicholas placed it in here just for me. He understands my obsessions.

Nicholas pulls a gun from his pocket and points it directly at Edgar.

"The documentation you all seem to favor states at this point I should remove your head with the sword of my ancestry. I find that far too messy though. I'm going to deviate from the rules a little bit and try something new." The corner of his lip lifts into a devilish smile. He's the King of Oakfield, now, and he's cleaning out the trash. I shut my eyes, so I can allow my hearing senses to take over.

The gun fires as Edgar whimpers for his life. Well, at least, I think that's what he's doing because with no tongue, it's a little hard to understand him. I hear his skull crack and then silence. The smell of death invades my nostrils, and I open my eyes again. Edgar Rushbrooke is dead. Amelia can finally rest in peace. I've never felt so happy until the mess in the room hits me, and my need for cleanliness starts to itch at my skin.

Nicholas places his gun away and comes over to me. He picks up a towel to wipe his hands clean before tapping me on the shoulder.

"Don't worry. I've got a friend Matthew Carter who's ex MI-5. Since he found out what I've been doing, he's been more than happy to help with cleanups. We don't have to do it."

I laugh, looking back toward the dead man now slumped over in his chair.

I shift in my seat as the learning of my youth comes flooding back to me. Intricate details of the human body recollected in a photographic memory.

"Did you know the large intestine is bigger than the smaller one?" I ask Nicholas

"I remember something about that from my biology lessons at school. I preferred the sex education part, though. That stayed with me a good deal longer." He winks at me. "I enjoyed heading over to the nearby girl's school after lessons to show them just what I'd learned."

"How Victoria puts up with you, I'll never know?" I roll my eyes and look back at the body.

"We're still in the honeymoon stage. I'm sure it won't last. Then, I'll just have to keep fucking her, so she's too tired to care." Nicholas responds.

"Really don't need to know that." I push myself up from the seat and walk over to where Edgar is. The floor is covered in blood, and I can hear it squelch under the boots I'm wearing. The intestines always fascinated me as a child–the fact an organ that long could fit inside us. I place my hands over where they rest in my own body.

"William?" Nicholas is beside me. His voice full of concern. We've always been close, and he's protective of me–sometimes to the extreme. I'm the same with him, though. "What is it?"

"I want to see them." I tell him.

"See what?" he asks, his brows furrowing together.

"The intestines. This may be the only chance I get. I have to know if they really are as long as all the books say. Is that bad?"

His eyes flick over to Edgar. "It's not exactly normal, but I know you've always had an interest in the human body. My credit card knew it when you spent over five hundred pounds on books about the human body, as well as a massive skeleton and a muscle statue."

"I hope you're not bad-mouthing Indiana Bones and Macho Man."

"Never!" Nicholas chuckles and goes over to a table in the corner of the room. "Get him out of the chair and lay him down."

I look up at my brother and swipe my head, tap my foot, and bang my fingers.

"Are you sure?"

"I've got no interest in what happens to this man. You can cut him up into little pieces if you want. Examine his heart, lungs, and whatever else you want to look at. He can be turned into dog food for all I care. Edgar's in hell, now, and I'm not returning him to his family to bury. He doesn't deserve our respect." He hands me the knife. "You want to do it, or shall I?"

I look at the knife handle and then at the body. My stomach lurches a little before settling as my excitement builds at the thought of what goodies lie under the covering of skin and muscle.

"You can do it. I'll put some gloves on and help lay out the intestines. Do we have anything to measure them with?"

"Over in that drawer, there's a tape measure." He nods his head toward a modern IKEA unit. It looks out of place in comparison with the abundance of antique furniture we have all over our house, but I guess it was specially purchased for this purpose and can be easily disposed of. Not worth risking a thirty-thousand-pound sideboard when you can use one costing less than twenty pounds. I pull the drawer open and rummage through the contents until I find what I'm looking for. When I turn back, Nicholas is already pulling the intestines out through the massive hole he's cut into Edgar's abdomen. I breathe deeply, my body fizzing with excitement. I'm sure I should be worried about the perverse pleasure I'm getting from seeing a man cut open with his guts spilling out, but I need to see it. I've been told I've been wrong all my life, so why should I try to act any differently now. I've been presented with this opportunity, and I'm not going to waste it.

Nicholas finishes pulling the intestines out and cuts them off. The human waste from the body spills out on to the floor, and he curses when it splatters on his shoes.

"Fuck." He grabs a cloth and wipes the mess off before throwing the towel into a nearby sink. This basement is specifically designed for the work we're undertaking, but it wasn't Nicholas who set it up. It's a remnant from my father's time.

"Sorry," I tell him.

"Not a problem, really. I'll disinfect them later. Now, how do you want me to do this?"

"I think we need to lay it out flat around the floor." I take hold of the end that's attached to the small intestine. This is the large intestine or colon to give its proper title." I tell Nicholas.

"Paradoxically that's the shorter one, right?" He places some medical gloves on his hands and takes the other end, leading to the anus, and helps to stretch it out.

"Yes. It should only be around five feet."

We place it down, and I get the tape measure, which confirms it is about the correct length. I put my fingers around the organ and squeeze. It feels squidgy to the touch.

"This has never been my favorite choice of meat." Nicholas screws his nose up. "You remember when Nurse made us eat tripe because it would be good for us."

"I remember you trying not to gag and throwing it out of the window at every available opportunity."

We pick up the small intestine and start the more substantial task of laying that out.

"I don't think even the dogs or foxes would've wanted it." He laughs, and I join him. We finish laying out the small intestine, and I measure it.

"It's twenty-five foot long. That's about average. They can get up to thirty-four feet. I check the width of it and notice it's bigger than the standard of an inch. "It's dilated."

"What?" Nicholas is at the sink, washing his hands.

"The intestine. Its width is greater than it should be."

"You are going to have to speak in dumb people terms, little brother." Nicholas dries his hands and picking up his phone, he quickly types out a message. I know it's to call in the cleanup crew.

"When the small intestine is like this, it's a sign something is wrong. I think he might have been sick, even dying. It's not good like this. He would have been in pain."

"Damn," Nicholas exclaims. "I should have left him in

pain. Mind you, I think we made sure he suffered enough. Amelia will be proud."

"She will." I smile as I think of the terrified girl I'd met. "It will give her peace."

"It will." Nicholas' face falls. I know the guilt of his part in Amelia's death weighs heavily on him. He suffers for it every day, and it's the reason he's trying to get rid of all the others who caused her torment.

"Come on," I say to him and wrap my arm around his shoulders. "Let's go shower and see that pretty wife of yours."

"A perfect plan."

As we leave the room, I turn back one final time and look at the intestines laid out neatly in a row, together. This is not normal. I know it. I can't help worrying about the effects of being confined away for so many years and what damage it may have inflicted on my soul.

CHAPTER TWO

TAMARA

My hands tap impatiently on the dividing screen of the black London taxi I'm traveling in. I swear this man could put his foot down if he wanted to, but he's deliberately driving slowly because he knows I need to be somewhere. I have to be at Oakfield Hall, but not today, not even yesterday. I needed to be there the day, all those months ago, when Nicholas Cavendish first set eyes on my best friend. I still can't believe she married the man. I swear he must have brainwashed her or something because I saw the state of her after she was handed over by her father to the Cavendish family. She had a brand burned into her skin by Nicholas himself, for fuck's sake. How can you fall in love with a man who does that? No, he's definitely brainwashed her.

I lean forward in my seat to speak to the driver, "Any chance we can go a little bit quicker. I really need to get to Oakfield Hall. It's very important."

"Sorry, Miss." The middle-aged cabbie, with grey flecks all over his hair,

waves his hand in the air. "The roads are icy after the 'eavy frost this morning. It's making 'em difficult to pass through because nobody salts 'em. Too many private lanes, you see. If you ask me, the Duke needs to look at gettin' some of his staff to make sure the roads are safe. It's dangerous. If you weren't a lass on 'er own, I'd 'ave made you walk the last bit. I don't know what's down the side of 'em ditches. One wrong turn of my wheel, and we'd be down one. You a friend of the Duke? You need to tell 'im. Make it safer for us all out 'ere."

"I know the Duke, well sort of. My best friend is married to him." I manage to get out from between gritted teeth. If we don't get to Oakfield Hall soon, then woman alone or not, I'm going to get out of this cab and walk. The roads are barely icy because the sun's been on them, and the frost melted ages ago.

"Lady Victoria?" The cabbie slows down even further, so he can continue our conversation.

I don't want to reply to him because I know he'll increase his speed if I don't engage in conversation, but I've been brought up to have good manners, and I know it's rude not to respond. "Yes." I keep my answer short, though, in the hope he'll go faster.

"Lovely lady she is. I live around these parts, so I've seen 'er a few times in the village. That 'usband of 'ers is never far behind, though. I'm not sure about the Cavendish family."

The driver indicates left while speaking and turns off the lane up what appears to be a long driveway. I hold my breath, hoping we may have finally arrived. "The father dying so young then the other brother showing up out of nowhere like that. You 'ave to wonder where 'e's been all these years. It's a mystery. Your friend say anything to you about it?"

A massive mansion looms up ahead, and I've never been so grateful to see a place, even knowing what's happened behind its walls.

"I'm afraid not." I pull my wallet out as the driver pulls his cab to a halt. He presses the buttons to stop the clock and to give me the total for our ride. I can tell by the way he's huffing he's not happy and wanted some gossip from me to spread around the black cab network in London. Anything remotely associated with aristocracy is the '*bread and butter*' of his industry. I'm sure by the time the tale of my journey has been spun a few times, he will've had the Duke himself instead of me in the back of the cab.

"That'll be forty-five pounds and twenty pence," he tells me, and I try not to let my stomach turn at the exorbitant cost. I could have caught a train closer to Oakfield and then taken a taxi the last few miles, but it would've taken so much longer. I just want to see my friend and check she's alright. I bring out two twenty-pound notes and a ten and hand them to him.

"Keep the change." I smile, grabbing my small suitcase from the cab floor and jumping out of the vehicle.

"Thanks, love," the cabbie calls behind me, but I'm already making my way up the steps of the imposing mansion. Although I grew up with Victoria in a large house, there's something about this one that sends chills down my spine, and I can't help wondering if it's because of the horrifying historical events that have occurred behind its closed front door.

Using the ornate iron knocker, I bang loudly to gain entrance. A butler appears immediately and ushers me into a side room off the main entrance. He takes my name and tells me he will inform the Duke and Duchess of my arrival before leaving me alone. My hands are shaking so badly I have to clasp them together to stop. I need to see my friend I have to know she's ok. I hear a scream from somewhere in the house, and I know it's Victoria. I'm out of the room and following the sound when I hear my name called.

"Tamara." The shout comes as my friend flies down the grand staircase and straight into my arms. She's half dressed with her crisp white shirt ripped at the front. Then a man appears behind her, fumbling with the flies of his trousers clearly trying to fasten them as he descends the stairs. I see red. Was he raping my friend? Pushing Victoria aside, I go to meet him. I pull my fist back and slam it directly into his face.

"How dare you? You disgust me. You're a sick, sick pervert. If I had a knife, I would remove your balls and dick before feeding them to you." Bringing my knee up this time, I send it straight into his groin area, and he curls up in agony.

"Tamara, what the fuck are you doing?" Victoria screams out behind me and comes to the side of the man who's hunched over and rubbing his groin.

I grab her hand and pull her away, but she digs her feet into the carpeted flooring.

"We are leaving now," I snap, but my best friend tries to squirm from my hold.

"Tamara, have you gone insane?"

"No, but I'm beginning to think that whatever he's done to you has left you seriously in need of a doctor."

"He's not done anything to me."

"He forced you into a marriage. He branded you!" I hold my hand out as if to say, 'are you really that blind'.

"He did nothing of the sort," she replies in irritation.

I raise a knowing eyebrow at her.

"Alright, yes he branded me, but that was under his father's orders."

"Didn't he have a mind of his own?" I place my hands on my hips while Victoria goes back to her husband and starts to rub his groin area, but he pushes her hand away with a shake of his head. I secretly hope he gets himself hard, so that the bruised flesh stretches, and it hurts him even more. He looks up at me, and I glare at him with such a venomous look, I suspect it could kill if I possessed magical powers.

"It was different. Tamara, please. Listen to me. I love him."

I roll my eyes.

"Stockholm Syndrome," I tell her, but she shakes her head.

"No, true love. A 'til death do us part kind of love...because I couldn't survive without him kind of love."

A laugh comes from the top of the stairs, and we all turn our heads to look up. A handsome man stands there. My breath catches at the sharp cut of his jaw, which is littered with stubble. He's not dressed as formally as Nicholas but wears a forest green polo shirt and black jeans. His strong thighs are accentuated by the style of pants he's wearing. I lick my lips. He has a similar look to Nicholas, and I guess this must be his brother, William. He's the one who saved Victoria when the evil Scotsman tried to rape and murder her. I push past Nicholas and Victoria and run up the stairs to meet him. Throwing my arms around him, I pull him to me and give him a kiss on the cheek.

"Thank you, thank you," I tell him. "I can never repay you for saving my best friend. You're a good man."

Turning back around again, I scowl at Nicholas who in turn looks at Victoria as if to ask 'why do I get the crap kicked out of me, and my brother gets affection? Women are nuts'. He's the reason my friend suffered as she did, and it'll be a cold day in hell before I trust him.

"Enough, Tamara." Victoria takes her husband's arm and leads him into the side room I'd just come from. William links his arm through mine and assists me down the stairs, so we can follow them.

"He's really not that bad. My father was an evil man. It took Nicholas a little while to step out from under his control. He loves Victoria intensely and will do anything for her–he worships the ground she walks on. You really don't have to worry about her safety."

"Really?" I roll my eyes again. I was well known for doing it at university when people annoyed me. It's a habit I picked up from my mother–she was always doing it when I was younger. My mother is a placid person, most of the time, but get her onto a subject that irritates her, and her eyes start rolling around like a merry-go-round. "So why is her shirt all ripped?...and he was putting himself back in his trousers when I first saw him."

"Sex," William replies bluntly.

"I'm sorry?" I quiz in confusion.

"They were about to have sex. They do it most days... numerous times. I've bought a pair of headphones to escape the noise. They're like rabbits." Letting go of my arm as we walk into the room, he makes a circle with the index finger and thumb of his right hand and then sticks the index finger of his left hand through the middle of the circle. "All the time…like bunnies. Nicholas puts his dick in Victoria's pussy a lot."

My mouth falls open.

"William!" Nicholas and Victoria both chastise him at the same time.

"Inappropriate conversation in public," Nicholas reminds him.

William shrugs. "But it's true!"

Nicholas is sitting in an old leather arm chair while Victoria having collected ice out of a bucket in the corner of the room is now walking back toward her husband, clearly, he needs something to reduce the swelling I caused earlier with my knee.

"I know, but we don't say things like that in front of guests," Nicholas informs him.

"But she's not a guest. She's Victoria's best friend, and girls are always gossiping. I'm sure she knows all about the size of your dick, and what you can do with it."

"William, please!" My friend's shocked response comes as she unceremoniously drops the ice, now wrapped in a towel, into her husband's lap. When I look at her, a rosy tint spreads across her cheeks.

I suppress a little giggle at how embarrassed my best friend looks. We've not spoken a great deal since she was given by her father to the Cavendish family. It's one of the reasons I've been so worried. But now, taking the time to look at her, and the way she's interacting with Nicholas, it would be impossible not to see the love she has for him. Having removed the ice from her husband's lap, she's now tenderly stroking his face while he tries to get comfortable in the chair. My temper and worry for my friend got the better of me, and I didn't allow her to explain.

"I'm sorry," I admit with a wave of my hand toward Nicholas. I lower my head to look down guiltily at the ground. "Having been told by Victoria about everything that happened, I couldn't get past the bad stuff to see you two are happy together. I hope I've not permanently damaged anything...down there?"

I bite my lip and gesture toward his male parts. Nicholas stands and comes over to me, limping slightly, and formally holds his hand out to me, which I take and shake.

"Victoria wasn't always my first priority, and what you just did to me was a well-deserved punishment. But I can assure you Victoria's my world, now. I'll do anything to protect her." He shuffles from side to side as if to test out the discomfort he's still experiencing. "I think I'll be alright in a few hours. As William so eloquently commented earlier, my wife and I are in the honeymoon stage, and I can't disappoint her." He winks at me before pushing his brother along toward the door. "We'll go and arrange some food and drink. Leave you girls alone to catch up."

"Thank you." Victoria nods her head at him before coming up to me and pulling me into an embrace again.

"I really am sorry," I tell her.

"Like he said, he deserved it." She laughs. It's beautiful to hear and looking closely at her, for the first time, I can see how happy she truly is. She looks alive and free. I sniff and take in her rose scented perfume.

"Some things never change. Your favorite flower. I hope he buys you plenty."

"Everyday." She sniffs the air around me. "I see you haven't changed either... is that lily?"

"Of course."

Victoria leads me to take a seat on a chaise longue, overlooking the grounds of the house.

"Are you truly happy?" I ask her, just to confirm one final time.

"I've never been happier." Her reply blows away any lingering doubts I have, and we settle in for an afternoon of gossip and catching up on how very different her life has become.

CHAPTER THREE

WILLIAM

"Dinner is served," my brother's new butler, Alfred, announces, and I take Tamara's arm to escort her into the dining hall. We don't always eat like this. I normally sit in the kitchen with the chef and talk to him. He's lived an interesting life and cooked for a variety of people all over the world. Nicholas and Victoria usually eat at a smaller table in the cozy dining room, but Victoria wants to show her friend that she's truly happy, and so we're going all out with the grand gesture for our guest. Victoria is dressed in a flowing gown, and Nicholas is dressed in full evening attire. I've even dressed up, a bit, for the occasion. Instead of my usual green t-shirt,

I've put on a formal shirt with a green tie and a black suit. It feels strange to wear something so restrictive. When my father was alive, I'd had to dress up for special occasions, but they were few and far between and never in polite society. I was too much of an embarrassment to him with my silly movements and inability to filter what I said. I swipe at my ear and then continue with my tapping routine. Tamara looks up at me.

"Are you alright?" she asks as a loose tendril of her long, jet-black hair falls out from the elaborate hairstyle she has pulled her locks into. I know Tamara's mother is of mixed heritage with African and Saxon ancestry, and these origins have combined in Tamara to give her an exotic beauty she shares with many a famous movie star or even a royal wife. She's dressed in a bright teal dress, stopping just above the knee, and black heels that make her legs seem like they go on forever.

"It feels a bit strange, wearing a formal outfit. I'm not used to it."

"I thought you would've been dressed like this for most of your life?"

"No. I didn't really eat dinner with my father and brother." I can feel my need to tic getting more urgent, and I swipe over my face and tap a few times. Tamara looks up at me, and then holds her hand out for me to take her arm. I do so and lead her into the dining room behind Nicholas and Victoria.

"I had a friend at university who struggled with formal occasions and preferred his own company. My university was a prestigious one, and we frequently had to dine in formal attire. He hated it, so I told him to imagine he was at home in his PJs and having a microwave meal. Those around him were doing just the same, and he didn't need to worry about the formality."

I can't stop the 'hmm' that escapes my mouth. It's the beginning of a thought I probably shouldn't voice, but one I know is going to spill from my lips anyway.

"I don't wear PJs."

Tamara laughs.

"Is this one of those pretend pair of PJs occasions?" I ask. My brain is wired differently to everyone else, and sometimes it takes throwaway comments far too literally.

"It is, but don't worry, I don't wear anything to bed either."

My thoughts go down a whole different route at that comment. Quickly pulling out her seat, I help Tamara to sit at the table before my dick manages to find its way out of my pants. I take my own place next to my brother who's at the head of the table with Victoria seated on his other side, and Tamara's next to her. The dining table is of carved, vintage oak and can seat many more people than just the four of us. We probably look a bit silly eating at this massive table when there are so few of us, but I can sense the anxiety emanating from Victoria with the need to please her friend and to reassure Tamara she has a happy life with Nicholas.

The butler and a maid appear and start to serve us the first course. It's a fiddly dish involving scallops and cauliflower purée. I'm aware of this because I was in the kitchen earlier when the chef was preparing everything, following Victoria's request for something fancy. I would've preferred baked beans on toast with a sprinkling of cheddar cheese, but that isn't considered the height of gastronomy, apparently.

Picking up my fork, I dig into the scallop and pop it in my mouth. It actually tastes good– I'm getting a little hint of curry flavor from it, but it doesn't overpower the taste of the mollusk. It's really tasty. I look over to Tamara and see her pushing it to the side of the plate.

"Don't you like it?" I ask, and Victoria looks over from her conversation with Nicholas to her friend.

"Tamara?" She frowns.

"I'm not the biggest scallop fan. We had some once, and they left me sick for a few days afterward. I've been put off eating them ever since."

Victoria lets out a heavy sigh.

"I knew it would go wrong"–tears pool in her eyes– "I told you." She turns back to my brother who's already getting out of his chair and coming to wrap his arms around his emotional wife.

"It's only the first course. It doesn't matter," Nicholas reassures Victoria and at the same time waves the butler over. "Can you ask chef for something different for Miss Bennett, please?"

"At once, sir." He picks up Tamara's plate, but she tries to stop him.

"Please, don't worry. Everyone has nearly finished. I'll just wait for the next course."

The butler hovers with the plate, waiting for Nicholas to instruct him on how to proceed.

"It's alright, Alfred. Take all the plates and bring the main course. It's lamb. Is that alright?" Nicholas smiles reassuringly at Tamara.

"My favorite," she responds, and the butler clears the table. "Victoria, please don't worry. I'm over my temper tantrum with Nicholas. I can see you love him, and he loves you. You don't have to impress me or get yourself stressed. I would've been just as happy with our childhood dinner of pizza and cupcakes in front of the TV."

"I'm sorry." Victoria leans over and brings her friend into an embrace. "I do love Nicholas... I promise you. He's doing so much to correct the past wrongs of his family. Only today, he prevented a really nasty man from ever hurting anyone again."

Nicholas clears his throat with a deep cough. "Possibly not a conversation we should have at the dinner table."

I can't help but laugh. "I don't know...in some countries, the organs we played around with today are considered to be delicacies."

Tamara pales, and I realize instantly I've said too much.

"What...What do you mean?" she stutters.

"Nothing," both Nicholas and I reply at the same time. My brother gives me a scowl, which says I need to keep my mouth shut about other aspects of our afternoon excursion.

"No." Victoria, reaches out and takes her husband's hand in her own and squeezes it. "I want Tamara to know everything. It's the only way she can make an informed decision about whether she'll help us or not. She's a fantastic lawyer, Nicholas. She's still learning, but what we are trying to achieve will give her great experience in so many aspects."

"I'm not sure I like the sound of this, not when it's combined with the term organs." Tamara worries the edge of her lip with her teeth, and I can't help but think I'd like to sink my own teeth into that plump part of her flesh. What the hell is going on with me, at the moment? Every time I look at this woman, I start imagining her in a sexual way. I don't do this. Women are brought to me, I do what I need to, to get off, and then they're taken away again. I don't do feelings...they're too complicated, and heaven knows, the thoughts running through my head don't need any additional distractions. I look away from her and drain my elaborate wine glass, which had been full of the finest Chardonnay.

"I've told you a lot about what happened when my father handed me over to Nicholas. I also mentioned a girl called

Amelia to you," Victoria says, turning her chair to face her friend. At this, Nicholas gets to his feet and walks over to take a protective stance at the door used by the staff. Our employees know of our exploits, but they don't need to be discussed openly in front of them.

"I remember. She died during one of the trials. You said that her father had abused her since she was born."

"Yes, he'd forced her to practice completing the trials that I had to endure. She didn't just do them once... he made her repeat them several times, so she would be prepared for whatever Nicholas threw at her. He raped, abused, and degraded his own daughter. I hadn't realized the full extent of the fragile state of Amelia's mind until her last moments. The only task she hadn't completed was to kill a man, and when confronted in the trials with having to commit murder, she simply couldn't. It was the one that broke her." Victoria pauses and wipes a tear from her eye as I look over to my brother. His head is bowed, and the guilt of Amelia's death causes his shoulders to slump. It's one of his biggest regrets that he couldn't save her. Her death will haunt him until the day he dies. I'd watched the girl numerous times during the trials, though, and I know she was beyond saving. Death gave her the peace she needed, allowing her to escape from the prison her mind had become. Putting a gun in her hand was the biggest favor Nicholas could have done for her.

"How can a father do that to his own daughter?" Tamara sits in her chair stunned. Her mouth has fallen slightly open, and confusion glistens in her eyes. "I just don't understand it."

"I don't think anyone does." Victoria dabs away another tear.

"Sometimes, people just have the devil in them. They remain completely unaffected by the damage their wicked actions cause other people. There is no good in them. Evil is a disease that riddles their entire being." I push my chair back and come to kneel between the girls. "My father had it, and Amelia's father was the same."

"And my father has it," Victoria adds.

Tamara lets out a long, slow breath. The realization of what has happened dawning on her. She looks at me.

"You killed your father when he tried to kill Nicholas and Victoria."

"Yes," I reply without regret.

Tamara looks over her shoulder at Nicholas.

"You killed Amelia's father."

Nicholas nods before replying.

"He died in agony, and his body was given no last rites or ceremony. His death was deserved for the abuses he inflicted on his daughter."

"But you had no right..." Tamara starts to lecture, but Nicholas puts his hand up to halt her.

"I may not have had the right to take his life, but he certainly lost the privilege of breathing with his actions toward his daughter. Too many people have been hurt, killed, or maimed by this society since its inception. I'm the ruler of it now, and I'll not rest until it's cleaned of all those who would seek to destroy a human life for power, monetary gain, or simply for sexual gratification. That is the world my father created. People who treated women like slaves. They abused them to the point they were unrecognizable as a human and then put a bullet in their heads. I couldn't save Amelia, but I will prevent this from happening again in my name. The Duke of Oakfield will no longer be synonymous with evil. He will be a loving husband, father, and ruler of a society helping to empower women."

"Why didn't you go to the police with the evidence of what Amelia's father had done?" Tamara asks, and I have to chuckle a little at her faith in the law. You can tell she is new to her profession and still believes in the honesty of all those working in it.

"Because the Commissioner of the Metropolitan Police was an active member of the society." Victoria says as she stands up from her seat at the dining room table.

"What!" Tamara exclaims, and her mouth opens and closes like a fish, trying to find sense in what she's hearing. "I can't... He can't...What?"

Nicholas comes to his wife's side and wraps an arm around her tiny waist.

"His wife suffered a stillbirth of a baby girl when Viscountess Hamilton was pregnant with my wife. If the child had been born alive, then she would have become my property on my thirtieth birthday. She would have suffered the same fate as the other girls I was given. I can only be thankful to god for not allowing another woman to experience the torment the others endured."

Tamara looks down at the floor, and I can see tears forming in her eyes. Reaching out, I take her hand in mine – it's warm to the touch, despite the chill in the air, resulting from her stark realization regarding the malevolence of some people in positions of respect and trust.

"How can they get away with this?" Tamara asks.

"They have the power," I respond. "It's the reason no one questioned the fact I disappeared after my autism diagnosis."

"I can't understand this. It's too much."

"It's a lot to take in," Victoria offers with sincerity and concern for her friend.

"What did you do to Amelia's father?" Tamara asks.

"No details," I tell her.

"Please. I need to know."

I look up to Nicholas, and he nods, affirming I can give her more details.

"I'm going to take Victoria to freshen up. I'll ask for dinner to be brought into the lounge. We can eat it in front of the TV." Nicholas places his hand on my shoulder before leaving with an arm wrapped around his wife to support her.

"William," Tamara pleads with me. "If I'm going to be here and get involved, I need full details of what you are doing. I want to help Victoria in any way I can. She's my life...my best friend, but everything is so scary, and I know nothing of this life. It's dark, horrifying, and alien to me."

"I know." I pull myself up and take a seat on Victoria's vacated chair. Scraping it along the wooden floor, I bring it nearer to Tamara, so I can still keep a hold of her hand while I talk to her.

"Nicholas and I captured Amelia's father and tortured him. We made him suffer by cutting off any distinguishing marks he had: moles that sort of thing. We removed his fingers, toes, and masculine parts before killing him. He needed to die that way to allow Amelia to rest in peace."

Tamara gasps and pulling away from me, she looks down at my hands in horror.

"You did it yourself? How can you do that to another human? Why not order someone else to do it?"

"I guess I have some of my father's darkness in me. I can't explain it. I wish I could. I understand if you want to leave here now and never come back. We won't stop you."

"Will he be the last one to die?" she asks with a quivering of her bottom lip

"I can't promise you that. I don't know what Nicholas wants to do with Viscount Hamilton."

"Victoria's father?" She gasps, bringing her hand to her mouth.

"Yes. He gave Victoria to Nicholas. Although he behaved better than the other fathers. At least he kept Victoria protected while she was growing up rather than abuse her. We will ensure he is ruined for his part in the society, but he's not as bad as some."

"These are people's lives you are playing with. Taking things into your own hands like God." I can see she's struggling to understand the motivation behind our actions. This evil world has only been revealed to her through tales of darkness. It's never been something she's experienced, felt, or thought about. She hasn't lived a life like the one Nicholas, Victoria, and I have endured.

"I wish I could explain it better to you. Victoria's father bought a girl during the trials. We've not seen or heard from her since that day. We don't know if she's alive or dead. He told us she was for Victoria's brother to marry, but as far as we are aware, he's still single. There is so much more going on, Tamara. These people are bad men. If they learn you are involved with us, they'll take, rape, and abuse you until the pain is so great that death is the only way out of the suffering. This is why we take the law into our own hands. Why we do what is necessary to put an end to the society we grew up in. It's the only way in our eyes. The people we are talking about are beyond the law in so many ways, but using what we know, we can restrict them and ruin them, so they can never rise again. The police chief is corrupt, so we'll find some incriminating evidence and use the law against him. Please, we don't want to kill anyone else unless they truly deserve it. That's why we need your help."

"I don't know. I'm still learning. I don't have the clout you think I do. I've not even completed the bar yet."

I shake my head.

"It doesn't matter," I reassure her. "Faith in your abilities is all you need. Just as Nicholas and I have in ours, even if our skills are a little different. This society's influence reaches everywhere... we need to destroy it!"

"I need to think about all this. Try to get my head around the truth that if I help you, then I'll have to look past the fact you and your brother kill people. It's not something I've been trained for or ever could be." When Tamara stands, I let go of her hand, and she walks toward the door.

"I understand." I remain seated. "Would you like food sent to your room?"

"No," she says as she turns to face me. "I want to talk to Victoria some more. I need to understand exactly what she went through. I've heard the pain in her voice as we've spoken about her experiences, but I need to also see it expressed in her face, visually, the way you and Nicholas have."

Pushing to my feet, I come to stand before her.

"I promise you, if there were any other way, I wouldn't do this either. The only reason it doesn't bother me more is because, I fear, I've been damaged due to the years of being in total seclusion."

"It hasn't damaged you, William. You showed the kindness within you by protecting and helping those girls as much as you could." She leans up and presses a chaste kiss to my cheek. "You helped save my best friend. I owe you silence and respect just for that, let alone for everything else you've told me today."

Bowing my head to her, I watch her turn to leave. Those familiar urges of sexual need rise within me again. I need to get this under control if we are to work together. Bad thoughts are what I need to focus on. My father... that should be enough to dampen any ardor.

Tamara gasps, drawing me out of my thoughts.

"What is it?" I step forward.

"My mother?"

It takes me a few moments to register who her mother is, and what she's asking.

"Nicholas has checked on her, and she's safe, as far as we're aware. She believes Victoria fell for Nicholas in the conventional way. Victoria has tried to get her to come and work here, but she refused out of loyalty to the Hamilton's."

"I have to see her." Tamara's eyebrows draw together. I can feel the fear rippling from her now. "Please, William. I have to make sure she's alright. If you say Lord Hamilton has a woman held captive and gave away Victoria in the manner he did, then she could be in danger. I need to check to make certain she's unaware of everything. She's all I have. I don't know who my father is. Please."

"Ok, you can go see her, but I'm going to come with you."

"What? You can't."

I take hold of Tamara's hand, probably a little too tightly, but the urge to protect her is surging through my body like a runaway freight train on steroids. I won't let anything happen to her.

"You want to see your mother, then I'm coming with you. No arguments."

CHAPTER FOUR

TAMARA

The chauffeur opens the door for me while William comes around and offers me his hand to hold, so I can ease myself with ladylike dignity into the car. William's palms are clammy, and when he comes to sit beside me, I can see the trepidation etched on his handsome face. His jawline is square, dotted with the stubble of a day-old growth, and his dark brown hair is trimmed short at the sides and shaggy on top. His brother has the air of pristine grooming, but William is more natural. He's the type of person who can roll out of bed, have a quick wash, clean their teeth, and look catwalk ready. At the moment, though, he looks ready to climb out of his own skin. His left hand is flicking at his ear, then the top of his head while his legs bounce up and down in a rhythm known only to him.

"William,"–I reach out to take his right hand– "Is everything ok?"

He gives me a wry smile.

"You can talk to me," I offer a little more reassurance, but he won't look me in the eye.

"The world moves so fast in a car," he says, staring out of the window. Turning my own head to observe the lush green fields of the countryside change into the densely populated suburbs of west London, I hold my breath while we weave down the once familiar streets toward my childhood home. I guess it does move fast, changing so quickly. The calmness I've been feeling disintegrates into nerves.

"You're not used to traveling like this, are you?" I ask. Victoria has told me a great deal about William. For most of his twenty-eight years, he's been hidden away, rarely leaving his bedroom let alone his home. To suddenly have all this freedom must make him feel agoraphobic as the intensity of the different sights, sounds, and smells overwhelm him. I'm aware of his autism diagnosis and how that can heighten his senses in comparison to those not on the spectrum, leaving him with a fear of unknown danger in these sorts of situations.

"No. I've been in a car only a handful of times in my life, and I can't drive one." He looks toward the driver who is indicating to make a right turn. William's eyes narrow with the ticking of the indicator as if the noise is too loud for him even though it's barely audible to me. "The first time I left with Victoria to rescue Nicholas, I didn't really think about what I was doing other than getting to my brother. But the second time, they had to virtually tranquilize me to get me to our destination…there's too much stimulation. I don't think I want to drive a car. I'd prefer to have my driver do it. With all the noises and movement, it's a lot to concentrate on, and even though it's easing, I still feel nervous."

"I can understand that. I don't like driving in London anyway. The drivers are too unpredictable. They could turn left while indicating right…I've had that happen to me before. It's not something you should be scared of, though. Sometimes, car journeys can be beautiful, and at other times insightful. You see different things, which can help you learn and study the world we're living in. For example, take the fields we just drove by… at the moment they are green, but travel the same road in summer, and they will be scorched yellow with the heat of the sun."

I stretch out my arm and point to some buildings being constructed. They are halfway to completion, and workmen are sitting on the top of the scaffolding with steaming cups of tea or maybe coffee. "Look at those buildings as well. The last time I came down here there was an old run-down factory from the seventies. It wasn't really in keeping with the area, so they decided to replace it with luxury accommodation for London's elite. I remember the Viscount being up in arms about the houses, wanting me to find some legal bylaw or statute to try and stop them being built. He wanted to have the factory demolished and the land converted into green woodland to match the forest area at the back of his property. Unfortunately, the council had a target they had to meet, and this was a perfect opportunity for them." I chuckle at the thought of Victoria's father being outwitted for once. When I hear William also emit a soft laugh, I look up at him. He points out of the window at another factory close to the entrance of the long driveway, leading to our destination.

"Maybe I should get Nicholas to purchase that factory and turn it into accommodation for London's not so elite!"

"Yes!" I exclaim with an evil snigger. "I know everything must be new and overstimulating to you, but truthfully, what you did for Nicholas and Victoria has already shown how strong you can be."

"Thank you." William replies and squeezes my hand in gratitude. "How do you want to play this with the Viscount, if we see him?"

My blood runs cold at the mention of the man who willingly sacrificed Victoria to hell on earth. I'm not entirely sure I'll be able to keep my calm around him. But for the sake of my mother, and a promise I made to Victoria in relation to keeping her brother, Theodore, in ignorance of all matters, I will bite my tongue. If I get time alone with him, though, he'll get a piece of my mind.

"I don't want Victoria to be upset, especially after her news this morning... she's too delicate." –William and I had left Victoria and Nicholas celebrating the news of a positive pregnancy test– "So I intend to be on my best behavior. I want to check on my mother and persuade her to leave with us. That is all."

"Good idea. I'll try to be on my best behavior as well. Though, my brain doesn't always listen to what I want."

I wink at him.

"I know. I've still not forgotten how you greeted me this morning."

"Hey, I brought you coffee." He smirks.

"Yes, and an appraisal of how beautiful my tits were looking."

"Well, they were."

We both laugh together, and the earlier tension in the car

dissipates just as we pull up to Viscount Hamilton's home. Once I thought the sun shone out of this place. It was my childhood home. Despite being a single mother with an unwanted pregnancy, Victoria's father allowed my mother to keep her job and even helped to educate me. I wanted for nothing, and he treated me just like a daughter. In some ways more so than Victoria who he always sheltered, never allowing her to forge her own path in the world. Now we know why! He was part of a secret society who placed no value upon women except for their usefulness as a bargaining chip. It's a betrayal I feel deeply in my heart, despite not being directly involved. He was like a surrogate father to me, and now it hurts to know the evil lying beneath the surface.

Before I've even realized that William has got out of the car, he's come around to my door and opened it. He holds his hand out for me, and I take it... I could get used to being treated like a lady. I've walked on the wild side at university for the last few years, but this feels nice, to be respected and cared for.

"You ready?" he asks.

I nod 'yes' and pull toward the servants' entrance at the rear of the building.

William coughs and refuses to move.

"Where are you going?" he questions and looks toward the main front door.

"I don't use that entrance unless I'm with Victoria."

His brows furrow together.

"I've been hidden away and forced to use secret doors for most of my life. I'm free now. I won't skulk away and use a back door when a perfectly good front entrance is available."

"I thought we weren't going to antagonize the Viscount."

"We're not, but we're also not going to hide away as if we

are nobodies. Technically, until Victoria and Nicholas have a child, I'm the Earl of Lullington: Nicholas' old title."

I look at William, and I swear I can hear him chuckling with an evil laugh. I know it's all in my head because he's standing there with an expressionless face. The only evidence of his mischief is the glint in his eye and the ever so slight curl to his lip as he strides off toward the front door. He rings the bell and Viscount Hamilton's butler, Marcus, opens up with a wide-eyed expression.

"Earl Lullington and Miss Tamara Bennett to see Ms. Elsie Bennett." William doesn't wait to be welcomed into the house. He pushes past the butler and into the hall. "Where is the receiving room? This way?" He points to a closed door to the left, which I know is the Viscount's personal lounge and not one he would want William and myself entering. The butler tries to get an answer out but is so stunned at the intrusion into his day that he stands there with his mouth hanging wide open.

"Come on, man. Did you not understand what I said? Do I need to repeat myself more slowly for you?"

"The Viscount is in his study," the butler exclaims in shock, having nothing better to say.

"I didn't ask to see his lordship. I requested Ms. Bennett. Please have her brought to me at once. I think I'll have a whiskey as well. Its past midday isn't it, Tamara?"

I look down at my watch, stunned by the change in William. It's like he's suddenly turned into his brother, and it's intriguing to watch.

"Yes. It's almost one."

"I think possibly a spot of lunch is in order as well then. I'm sure Ms. Bennett is entitled to a lunch hour."

A figure appears at the top of the stairs, her head poking

around the corner of a marbled pillar. I instantly recognize my mother who takes the stairs at a rapid pace to greet me as I race toward her.

"Tamara." She throws her arms around me. "I didn't know you were back. You should have called me. I would have asked permission to come to the station to get you. Where's all your luggage? In the taxi?"

The butler clears his throat with a loud cough and nods toward William. My mother's face instantly falls.

"Earl Lullington." She presents a small curtsy, but William waves his hand to tell her to stop. "The Duchess is she here?" my mother enquires and gulps...I wonder why?

"No, my sister-in-law is at home resting. She's had an eventful few months, and we discovered she's pregnant, this morning, so the Duke wants her to take it easy."

"You sure it's just resting." A new deep voice enters the conversation when Theodore, Victoria's brother, steps out of his father's lounge. The Viscount is behind him, and it takes all of my strength to stay rooted to the spot and not run forward and scratch his eyes out.

"Elsie, bring dear Tamara and the Earl in here. It will not do to keep them standing in the hallway like unwanted guests." The Viscount holds the door to his lounge open, and Theo steps out of the way to allow us through.

"Will you be alright, father?" I hear Theodore say with an icy tone.

"Yes, of course. Let me know what you find out."

"I will." Theodore disappears, and the Viscount follows us into the room.

"Was the purpose of your visit to bring us the joyful news of Victoria's pregnancy? Or was there something else?" The

Viscount's words are clipped, and we all stand around in the room on tenterhooks.

"Miss Bennett wanted to see her mother," William replies. He's like a totally different man from the person wracked with fear in the car. Now, he's confident and purposeful and stands up tall against his formidable foe. The Viscount shows no remorse for his actions. He must be aware I know the truth since I've seen Victoria and chosen to have William accompany me, but he wears the mask of a concerned father well.

"Of course, she does." The Viscount comes over to me and wraps his arms around me. He strokes my back and presses a kiss to my forehead. It has all the hallmarks of the tender fatherly display I would expect from him, but I can't help but feel cold and disgusted by it. "Tamara, I'm so proud of the results you achieved in your law exams. You put most of your class to shame, and the position you've secured at Wells and Partners is prestigious, to say the least. I'll have to see to it that all my legal affairs are transferred to the company in future."

William snorts and opens his mouth. He pauses, not saying anything before swiping at his ear and then his head. Viscount Hamilton steps away from me and looks toward William, warily.

"Is something wrong, Earl Lullington?"

"Nothing," William replies curtly and takes a seat, which allows everyone else in the room to also relax in comfort. The tension fills the room like helium trying to burst out of a balloon, but decorum is maintained at all times. This is how the upper classes do things. My mother remains standing. In this domain, she is staff and unless invited to sit, she'll not do so. Although I remain the daughter of a staff member, I'm finding it hard to behave in the manner my mother's position requires. All the respect I had for the man in front of me has gone.

"Mama, come sit with me," I tell her, and she widens her eyes toward the Viscount in concern.

"Elsie, join your daughter." The Viscount motions with a flick of his wrist, and that one action strengthens my resolve to take her back to Oakfield Hall with us.

My mother comes and sits beside me, and taking hold of her hand, I bring it into my lap. The room goes silent until the butler enters with a whiskey for William.

"Chef is preparing some sandwiches for our guests, my lord. Miss Bennett, may I get you a drink?"

"No thank you, Marcus." I reply, and we all fall back into quiet, again. William brings his whiskey to his mouth, takes a sip, and then places it down on the counter before standing and addressing the Viscount.

"Hamilton, I hear from Victoria that you have a beautiful winter rose garden. Maybe, you could show it to me, so I can pick one to take back to her. I'm afraid my parents were not as fond of the flower as your family. Our gardens are severely lacking in that particular bloom."

The Viscount reluctantly gets to his feet with a vicious glare toward William. The two leave the room, and I'm alone with my mother for the first time in almost a year.

"How is Victoria?" she asks.

"She's good. Very happy."

"Are you sure?" A line of worry mars her forehead. I take a moment to properly look at her. She has aged during the last year and has lost weight.

"Yes. She and Nicholas are really in love. He worships her." I take in a deep breath. "Mama, Victoria told me she asked you to come and work for her, but you said no. Do you know what happened to her?"

My mother gulps and tears start to form in her eyes.

"You do. Then, why not leave?"

"I can't." She pulls away from me and stands. Her eyes keep flicking to the door. "It's complicated. I have to stay here."

"Mama, please. I'm worried for you here."

"I'm safe."

"How can you be? You know what he did to Victoria. Her own father! He gave her away like she was nothing but a tool to advance his name. How can you bear to be here any longer?" I'm really confused. My mother has always been a strong woman, and someone I look up to. She's terrified, though. Her hands are fidgeting. "He's forcing you to stay here, isn't he? That's it, we're going!"

I jump up from my chair and taking her hand, I start pulling her toward the door.

"Tamara, please stop. You don't understand." She digs her heels in, but I'm stronger, and we're out into the hall before she has a chance to stop me.

"I understand perfectly. He's an evil man. I'm not going to allow you to stay in this house for another moment longer."

William and the Viscount appear in front of me. William's brows are furrowed together, and anger radiates from him. The Viscount has a smug smile on his face.

"You sick, sick man." I let go of my mother and stomp toward him. My hand raises of its own volition and slaps him hard across the face. He grabs it and yanks me toward him, so my body is flattened against his.

"You think I'm sick? You know nothing, little girl. You're staying with the devil himself…a man who branded five girls to prove his ownership of them."

"Only because he had no choice, and one of them was the daughter you knowingly gave to him," I spit back in his face.

William seems to come to life and pulls me away from the Viscount.

"Don't you dare touch her," William snarls as he pushes me behind him.

"Why would I want to do that when I have Joanna?" The Viscount laughs, and I see William pull his own fist back. I remember Victoria mentioning a missing girl called Joanna who'd been bought at an auction by the Viscount. This must be the woman he's referring to.

"No! William. He's not worth the trouble. We are going." I return to my mother and grab her hand. "You are coming with us, no arguments. I'll have William drag you to the car if I need to."

"Tamara, please don't do this. Please stay, we can all discuss this together," my mother whimpers.

"I won't spend another minute under his roof."

It's uncouth, but I turn and spit at the Viscount's feet as William takes my mother's other hand, and we drag her toward the front door. At the same moment, the butler appears with a tray of sandwiches but instantly turns around when he sees the confrontation going on.

"Why don't you tell her why you don't want to leave, Elsie? See if she wants you with her, then." The Viscount's evil laugh comes from behind us, and I feel a chill wash over my body.

"Tell her you knew all along what would happen to Victoria. That you were a part of my plan to keep her pure all those years. You watched her like a hawk. You helped dress her on the day I gave her to Nicholas, knowing full well what would happen to her. Tell her, Elsie. Tell her that if I'm evil, then so are you."

I'm vaguely aware of William letting go of my hand and heading back toward the Viscount. I don't look at what's happening, but the sounds of a fist meeting bone followed by a body crashing against the marble floor echo in the hallway. I should probably stop William, but all I can do is stare at my mother as she stands there repeating over and over again that she's sorry. I can't listen to it. I can't be hearing this.

"You knew," I cry.

"I'm sorry."

I try to say something else, but I have no words. My mother, the woman who I've always looked up to, knew what would happen to my best friend.

"Did he blackmail you to do it?" I ask as William appears at my side and wraps his hands around my waist. My mother looks to where the Viscount is lying flat out on the floor.

She shakes her head.

"It was my job."

My legs give way as my heart breaks, and William catches me. We leave my childhood home without a backward glance.

CHAPTER FIVE

WILLIAM

"Why, Mum? Why did you have to leave me?" I place my hand against the weathered headstone of my mother's grave. This is my place of calm, and it's exactly where I need to be, following our meeting with Viscount Hamilton. I left Tamara sobbing in Victoria's arms after learning that her mother knew what would happen to her friend. I can't even begin to understand the betrayal they must both be feeling. But it's Viscount Hamilton's mention of Joanna that has left me feeling unable to control my oddities: my hand swipes every few seconds around my ear and then on top of my head. I can tell I'm particularly anxious because my tongue darts out as well, swiping around my lips. In the cold air, I can already feel the skin getting sore. I can't stop my body's natural reactions – they are a part of me, and until I can rid my mind of my concerns about Joanna, they will remain. Why can't we find her? Nicholas and I have been searching everywhere we know the Viscount is linked to but have discovered nothing. It's as though she's vanished off the face of the Earth. Is she dead? No. Victoria insists her father told her Joanna was meant for her brother, but Theodore seems oblivious to the fact his father is hiding a poor girl somewhere. Maybe he's also involved? I'm sure Tamara never expected her mother to have been aware of Victoria's fate, let alone knowingly preparing her for it. The darkness we witnessed today is deep rooted and shows me Nicholas and I still have a long way to go to rid the world of the old Oakfield Society. There are still too many pockets hidden away, believing it's right to treat women as objects, fit only for their sickening desires. My ancestors including my father created a place for the monsters who dwell in the shadows to flourish. I just hope Nicholas and I can shed enough sunlight to destroy them all.

"It's so hard, Mama." I stroke her gravestone again and collapse down into the wet grass. "Everything is so different. Just being outside here in the fresh air. I never knew it could be so clean...no stale odors or dust. Why did he do this to me? Am I really that different?"

I shut my eyes and allow a memory from my youth to enter my head.

"Nicholas, don't be so stupid." *My father stands with his arms folded across his chest, looking down at my fourteen-year-old brother with a stern expression.*

"But, Your Grace, it's his birthday. Surely, he could join us for a little while. I'll look after him. He can sit next to me," Nicholas pleads.

"No."

"But..." Nicholas pleads again, and I look on from the shadows through a peephole into my brother's bedroom.

"If you ask me again, I will take him and lock him up in the tower just to shut you up." My father pulls my brother toward him, using his superior weight and height to impose greater discipline. I wish Nicholas would stop asking for me to join them for dinner. I don't mind that it's my twelfth birthday. I'm perfectly happy up in my room. It's quiet up there, and my brother brought me some new books to read today about all the different countries in the world. I'm beyond excited to start. He bought me a book of flags last year, and he takes great delight in trying to trip me up in naming them, but I know them all, even the obscure countries that nobody has ever really heard of such as Nauru, Benin, and Suriname. He even tried to fool me once by showing me the old flag for Venezuela, but luckily the book had shown me that as well. The books on countries will be amazing because I'll be able to learn more about them, their populations, languages, and all those sorts of amazing facts and figures. My tutor thinks it's a waste of time, but then he thinks it's a waste of time for me to be taught anything when I don't leave my room. It's not as though I'll ever be able to take any exams and gain qualifications, which I could use for a job in the future. My father says my job is just to behave and not embarrass him with my weird hand movements and inability to keep my mouth shut. I try so very hard not to say silly things, but I can't help it. If a thought pops into my head, I tell myself to keep it to inside, but it's as though there is a wire in my brain that isn't correctly plugged in, and I can't control the opening of my mouth and the words that come out.

All of a sudden, I'm brought out of my reflection when the door to the hidden passage I'm in is pulled open, and my father's hand reaches in and hauls me out to stand next to my brother.

"You're so strange you can't even hide quietly because of all the stupid foot tapping and hitting of things you do." He throws his hands up in the air. "Damn it, William, why do you have to be such an imbecile? You're a freak of nature. A result of your mother's addiction to drugs. I should have done us all a favor and had you terminated when I could have. But no, I wanted a spare in case anything happened to Nicholas and look how I was punished. The most stupid child in the world."

"I'm sorry," I mumble and try desperately to keep my hands and feet still, but I just can't do it. My left foot lifts and taps three times in quick succession on the floor.

"Damn it, William. Stop it. You're an intolerable embarrassment," my father curses at me.

Nicholas drops to his knees and tries to hold my foot still. He looks up at me with so much worry on his face – no fourteen-year-old should ever have that expression.

"I'm trying, Your Grace. I really am." My words catch in my throat with the effort I'm exerting, trying to keep still.

"It's all your mother's fault. You're just like her. Why was I lumbered with her winning the trials? I could have had any of the other women, but no, I get the wife who gives me one belligerent son, and one son who's a monster."

My hand swipes around my head really quickly, and my father's face reddens with so much anger that I know I've broken the last vestiges of his control.

He balls his fist and pulling it back, I feel the punch as he lands it hard on my face. His hands move to his belt, and I know what is coming next. He's tried so many times to beat the 'wrong' out of me. It never works, though. I'm what he says I am – a freakish monster. Nicholas is quick to his feet and blocks my father's path to me.

"Your Grace, please. I'll take him to his room. We'll keep him secreted away for the night, so he doesn't make an embarrassment of himself in front of your distinguished guests."

"Out of the way, Nicholas," my father scolds, and I see my brother go flying across the room. Before I have a chance to draw a breath, the biting leather of his belt cracks against the skin on my back. Even through the t-shirt I'm wearing, I can feel it burning my flesh. Nothing will stop my father now, until he's satisfied there's a chance that he's beaten the 'freak' out of me. It never works, though. I'll be back with my tics tomorrow, and there is nothing he can do about it. It's who I am, and why would I ever try to fit in when I was born to stand out? This is my future, and with each lash of the belt, I accept it.

"William?" The voice of an angel breaks me out of my reflection, and I realize I'm curled up on the floor as I would have been all those years ago, protecting as much of my body from the beating as I could. "What's wrong? Are you hurt?" Tamara appears at my side and instantly checks my forehead to see if I've a temperature.

"I'm alright." I tell her and pull myself upright. "A memory..." Climbing up, I look down at the ground to try and calm my rapidly beating heart.

"Do you want to talk about it?"

"No...Honestly, it's fine. How are you?" I question with genuine concern. She still looks tired, and the rims of her eyes are red from all the tears she's shed. My heart's still beating too quickly, but for another reason now. This one is an overwhelming need to protect the woman in front of me.

"You can talk to me," she says, deflecting the question from herself and centering it back to me.

"I was remembering my father's anger toward my quirks when I was a child. He used to beat me, thinking that maybe he could get rid of them that way. I was an embarrassment to him. It's why he hid me away for so many years."

"Your father was wrong. You're not an embarrassment, but he was. He was a shameful example of a man, especially being in such a respected position, and Viscount Hamilton continues to remain so even now. The way they treat women and children is disgusting. Actually no, scrap that…the way they treat most other human beings is wrong. William, for you to be the man you are today, and to have saved Victoria and Nicholas the way you did, proves that you've survived your father. You're stronger than everything he did to you. You suffered but came out on the other side, stronger. The way you carried me out of the Viscount's house today is more evidence of that. Yes, you may be quirky at times, but that's a part of you, and it makes me laugh. Please don't try to hide it…I like it. Plus, it makes my best friend blush when you talk about her sex life." Tamara giggles, and I can't help but smile at the enthusiasm she's exuding for me. Nicholas and, now, Victoria always support me in everything I do and who I am. Especially when I relax and don't try to rigidly control everything to the point where I'm tying myself in knots and making myself sick in the process. Tamara sees the real me as well, which makes me happy and surprises me.

Pushing up onto my feet, I brush off a few leaves that have stuck to my trousers. The day has warmed up, and the grass, which was frosty this morning has dried, so my trousers are not soaked through, maybe a little damp but nothing uncomfortable.

"Thank you." Taking Tamara's hand, I offer her respect for the way she has spoken to me. I protected her earlier today, and she's cared for me now. It's strange – I may have only known her for a little over twenty-four hours, but I feel more relaxed around her than anyone else. Tucking her under the crook of my arm, we both look back to my mother's gravestone.

"I'm sorry for the way she died." Tamara bows her head in respect. "It was cruel to have her taken away from you."

"To have us both taken away from her, really. She was never allowed to be a mother to Nicholas. He was always supposed to be my father's shadow. I'm just glad he was able to step out from under it."

"I'm sure she's up in heaven looking down proudly on her two sons, for everything you are achieving, and the way you are trying to undo all the wrongs of the past."

We both lower our heads to my mother's grave before making our way back to the house while I reflect on my answer.

"It won't be easy to right all the wrongs. We will find obstacles at every turn, but we won't stop trying. I don't know if there will be a happily ever after, but I'm going to try my hardest to find one."

We stop just inside the patio doors to the lounge. Tamara inclines her body so it's facing me, and I feel a heated sensation cascade through my skin. She really is the most beautiful woman I've ever seen. Her eyes spark with intelligence, mischief, and a caring nature all combined.

"I think you'll find your happy ending. The one thing I've learned is that you have determination."

"Determination. I like that. Determination to have what I want." I can't help but push my body closer to Tamara, and she reacts with a hitch of breath as her eyes filled with lust stare up at me.

"When all this is over, what else are you determined to have?"

"A wife," I reply instantly.

"And?" she questions with a playful bite to her lip.

"Children."

"How many?"

"A whole army. I never want any of them to not have a playmate if they want one."

"That's a lot!"

"You up for it?" I ask her before lowering my head and pressing my lips against her plump ones.

CHAPTER SIX

TAMARA

William Cavendish is kissing me! I think the world is tilting on its axis, and everything is becoming slightly surreal. I've only known him for just over twenty-four hours, but I already know in my heart I'm his. I can fight it all I want, but our souls have already become entangled with the emotions of what has happened to us. He sees himself as the poor boy abused by his father, but I see the strong man he's become – the lover who will respect me and worship me. I need this just as much as he does. Damn to hell the consequences.

Opening my mouth slightly, I allow his tongue entry to

ravage me with an urgency that seems to dominate his body. I'm pressed flat against the patio doors we entered through with the cold of the glass at my back, and his heat warming the front of my body. It's an assault on my senses, heightening the urgent need I have to feel his passion.

"William," I breathlessly utter into his mouth. He catches my words and responds by moaning out my name.

"Tamara."

He shifts his hips, and I feel the hardness at his groin as he strains to bring me to orgasm. If we don't find somewhere more private soon, I know he'll take me against this glass door for the world to see. I'm not sure Victoria and Nicholas will be impressed with having to clear a possible ass imprint off the glass panel.

"We need to go upstairs." I pull away but keep my gaze focused solely on him.

"You sure?" He brings his hand to my face and strokes the calloused pads of his fingers down my soft skin. "I'm different...I don't want to scare you."

"You are different in a beautiful way." My words are honest because he is. This isn't my first rodeo – I'll be the first to admit I was promiscuous at university. I'm pretty certain I nearly gave Victoria a heart attack when I told her about the orgy I participated in one night. As long as I was careful and set boundaries, then I was never one to think I needed to shy away from my sexual orientations. Yes, I've experimented: with men, women, both at the same time, and toys of different varieties. But William has seen the darker side of sex, and he's seen the pain and suffering it can bring. So when he says he's different, I'm not stupid – I know he's talking about his needs in bed and not his autism.

"If you want me to stop at any point, then you say, and I'll do so immediately," he offers me.

"Yes." Lowering my hand, I entwine it with his and lead him through the corridors of Oakfield Hall. My heart is thumping so loudly, and the need between my legs throbs with every step. As we walk, I can't help but hear the echoing screams of the many women who've been taken unwillingly to their fate in this place. The tables are finally turning.

On reaching my bedroom, I lead William in and go to sit on the bed. We're both silent as he remains stood at the doorway just staring at me. Finally, he turns and locks the door before striding over to me while at the same time removing his t-shirt. For someone who's been kept hidden away, he's clearly not been inactive over the years since his body is rippled with lines of taut muscles. His skin is slightly pale, especially against the dark tone of mine – ebony and ivory springs to mind when comparing us. I suck in a breath of lust at the sight of him.

"Stand up," he orders in a voice so deep and commanding it initially shocks me, and I jump straight to me feet. "I want to watch you undress."

William licks his lips while taking a seat in the plush Queen Anne chair in my room. He dwarfs the elegant chair with his size.

"Tamara, remove your clothes. Show me what I want to see."

With a shaking hand, I bring my fingers up to the top button of my teal blouse. My breaths are hitched while I slowly undo the fastenings and peel open the shirt to reveal a similar colored lace bra. William shifts in his seat, presumably to adjust the position of his hardness. I can't help but feel a little thrill of delight surge through my body that he likes what he sees.

"Tamara. The bra," he orders.

I drop my shirt to the floor and reach around my back to unclasp the fixings of my bra. I lower it carefully into my hands but keep the cups covering my breasts until the last second when I allow the gossamer material to fall and reveal myself to him.

"Fuck!" he exclaims. "Do you know how much I dreamed of them last night? I got off twice in the shower this morning just imagining my tongue wrapped around your flesh. They are even more beautiful, the nipples perter, and the shape more rounded than I even imagined."

"You played with yourself thinking of me?" I find myself shocked at the admission. I don't know why, because I found him instantly handsome from the first moment I saw him. I was just way too exhausted last night to contemplate using those visions to get myself off.

"You don't like me telling you that?" A line of worry creases William's forehead. "Tamara, I thought you'd have learned by now I say what I think, and that's both in and out of the bedroom. Around everyone else, I have to control it as much as I can, but here with you, I'm afraid, you're going to get everything." He rises to his feet and comes to stand directly in front of me. Grabbing the waistband of my jeans, he pulls me to him and grinds his hips into my waist. "Every dirty word...every commanding need. You will get it all from me. Say now if you want me to stop."

"No." The word spills from my lips before my brain has a second to even think about what he's just said to me. I need William between my thighs to relieve the urgent ache burning there.

"Good. Because I think we need to get these jeans off, now. I need to see that pussy I can smell getting ready to milk my big, hard cock."

Fuck! If he keeps up with the dirty talk, I'm going to come without any stimulation. In all my experiences, nobody has ever spoken to me like this before. It's intoxicating. His velvety tones, spilling filthy words about what he's going to do to me are almost like his fingers running directly over my clit.

William undoes the buttons of my jeans and pulls the fabric down over my thighs. He lowers his body, so he's kneeling in front of my pussy and takes a breath of air through his nose. I know he's sensing how much I want him.

"Please," I whimper... wanting...needing... something...anything.

"What do you want me to do, Tamara?" William looks up at me from under hooded eyelids, and when he hooks the tip of his finger in to my panties, I let out a groan of wanton desire.

"Please. Touch me."

"Touch you?" he says as he pulls my underwear down my thighs. I kick my shoes off to step out of my panties and my jeans. I'm naked before him, and every nerve ending in my body is tingling with desperation.

"Touch me." I repeat, and William presses his finger against my left arm.

"There you are...I touched you." He raises a playful eyebrow.

"No, not there."

He reaches up and swipes his finger over my shoulder.

"Please..." I cry, needing so much more.

"You have to tell me, Tamara. I need to know exactly what you want."

"Down there." I flick my eyes down between my thighs. Damn, what the hell is happening to me? I've taken the initiative before, but in front of William, it's like I've reverted back to an innocent virgin. He's messing with my brain, and it's making me so ready for him that I can feel wetness running down the inside of my thighs.

"You are going to have to elaborate, I'm afraid. I need full details. Remember, my brain's wired a little bit differently to others. They may know exactly what you want them to do to you, but I need to be told *explicitly*." The last word he says is so dark and demanding I groan and bring my own hand to my pussy. William stops it and lifts me effortlessly onto the bed.

"No," he snarls a warning that chills my blood but also sends electricity straight down to my clit. "You're with me. You don't touch yourself. I do all the touching." He looks around the room, and I wonder what for until I see him go for my dressing gown cord. Shit!

"William." My eyes go wide when he takes my left hand, and tying the cord around it, he threads the cord through the wire frame at the head of my bed before bringing it back down to secure my right hand with it. I'm trapped. "What are you doing?" I can sense the fear in my voice. The intensity of the situation is leaving me with little control. I'm not sure whether I'm willing to give up my say in the matter of our coupling. I don't have time to dwell on my worries, though, when once again William lowers himself down to my pussy and blows a long breath onto it. Fires ignite at the delicate current of warm air flowing over my heated flesh. He licks his lips and looks up at me. His eyes are dark, the pupils dilated so much he looks like the devil himself. Fuck! What am I getting myself into? With his dexterous tongue, William trails the length of my folds then flicks over the sensitive bundle of nerves at the peak. I'm writhing underneath him on the bed, wanting more. This is insane – I'm tied up beneath a man who's devouring my pussy and looks like Lucifer, and I want more. I want it all!

"William." I twist, thrusting my hips toward him, but he brings his hand up and pushes me down into the bed.

"No moving," he orders and goes back to eating me as if I was his last meal.

My body feels like it's on fire. I can barely make sense of anything but the throbbing between my thighs. I know I won't last long against this onslaught. His tongue is like a dangerous weapon, ridding me of all sense. I'm a wanton harlot, calling out for more, more, and even more.

The ricochet of an orgasm crashes into me when I least expect it. I thrash hard against the bindings on my restrained hands, but William is deft with a cord, and I can't pull them free. My body pulsates and jerks through every pleasurable sensation centered at my core. I've never had an orgasm like this before. It's taken over my whole body. My ears are ringing, my vision's blurry, and my limbs are shuddering of their own accord. Vaguely, I'm aware of William rising from the bed and divesting himself of the remainder of his clothes. I try to focus on his cock to prepare myself for what I know is about to come, but my head is still too cloudy with the aftermath of my orgasm. Something hard presses against my entrance, and I scream out with discomfort and overwhelming sensitivity as William pushes what feels like a massive dick into me.

"Oh God." I'm not religious, but at this very moment, if he can save me from this overload of pure, pleasurable sensation traveling through my body, I'm willing to attend church every Sunday for the rest of my life.

"Take me, Tamara." William says as he withdraws and then

slams back into me with a thrust that seems to go on forever. How fucking long is he? I can barely breathe.

William pulls all the way out this time, and I'm given a few seconds to collect my thoughts as he releases one end of the cord before flipping me onto my front and lifting me up onto my knees. He slams hard back into me, and in the back of my mind, I briefly think of contraception, but then that thought is lost with his animalistic thrusts.

"I need it rough, Tamara. I need to dominate you. I have to know for the next few days you'll feel me in every part of your body. I'm not normal, not even here. This is what he made me." William uses my body as his toy to get off, and my mind worries at the implications of all of this, but my body is so overridden with pleasurable sensations it's beyond caring.

"Made you?" I question as he wraps his hand around my neck.

"He made me this monster."

"Monster?" I'm so confused I can barely understand what is being said. Who's made him a monster? I want to question him more, but another orgasm slams into me like a freight train racing down a hill. I scream out his name, and William thrusts into me one final time as his hand around my neck tightens, and I feel the airflow into my lungs being constricted. A mild panic sets in, but William's roar of ecstasy and the warm spurts of his essence coating my insides, tip me over the edge, again. The world stands still, and I'm floating, suspended in a ball of pleasure as wave after wave of orgasm crashes into me. Eventually, I come back to earth, and we collapse down onto the bed together. I'm gasping for air – my neck hurts, and I need my hands freed. William pulls out of me, and I lament the loss despite the growing panic I'm experiencing.

"I...I...." William stutters. He unties my hands, and I turn around on the bed to face him. He's standing there covered in a fine sheen of sweat, his cock still half erect, and his chest heaving up and down at a rapid pace. He opens his mouth to say something but then slams it shut again. His hand comes up to his ear and swipes at it before going to his hair, and I listen for the foot taps, which quickly follow.

"William?" I move forward. My body jerks with aftershocks, feeling sore and overused from the exertion of our lovemaking.

His eyes flick to the full-length mirror, standing in the corner of the room. My gaze follows his and lands on the red ring forming around my neck from where he squeezed me during his orgasm. I look down to my wrists and see the burns on them, caused when I'd pulled hard on the fabric.

"I'm sorry." He flicks his ear again, and before I can respond, he's making his way butt naked out of the room, leaving me alone to stare at my well and truly fucked reflection in the mirror. I bring my hand up to my neck and touch the inflamed flesh there. He called himself a monster and said 'he' made him that way. It hits me what William meant – it was his father who taught him how to treat women. My stomach lurches, and I barely make it to my ensuite bathroom in time before I empty the contents into the toilet. If he's done this to me, what else has he done?

CHAPTER SEVEN

WILLIAM

*T*ap, Tap, stomp, stomp, swish, swish. I can do this – I can calm myself down before I do something even more stupid than I've just done by fucking Tamara. No, the fucking her wasn't wrong. It was beautiful – the best sex I've ever had. There was a connection between us until I went and spoiled it, allowing the monster within me to take over. My mind is a haze of confusion. Without showering or washing, I jump under the covers of my bed and pull the weighted blanket up to my neck. Instantly, I feel the plush fabric mold to my still naked form, enveloping me in its comforting embrace. I know it seems strange for a twenty-eight-year-old man to need a comfort blanket, but I really struggled trying to get to sleep until Nicholas read about these covers on the Autism UK website, recently. They're a new advancement in the fight against anxiety and the issues of ADHD and autism – specially designed to match the user's body weight, helping the user to feel grounded. I've slept so much better since he bought me the best one money can buy. When my mind is overstimulated, as it was before I climbed into my bed, it's the only thing that can prevent me from having a meltdown. And again, yes, I'm a twenty-eight-year-old man who has meltdowns and has been known to smash up his bedroom. It's part of my condition, but it isn't a daily occurrence. I need to fall asleep and try to forget everything that has happened today – chalk it up to a bad day and come back stronger tomorrow. Sometimes, that's all I can do when the world surrounding me borders on chaos in my mind.

A light knocking on my door draws me out of my reflection.

"William." Tamara's voice comes from the other side. Part of me doesn't want to let her in, but I know we need to discuss what happened between us. I sit up in the bed and pull the covers down to my chest. No point in being bashful, now. She's seen every part of me.

"Come in," I call back.

Opening the door slowly, Tamara peeps her head around the corner of it, and I instantly see she's been crying. I pat the bed, encouraging her to sit beside me. She looks at it, then me, and I can see the indecision on her face.

"I won't...I won't hurt you, again," I reassure her as she hesitantly comes to sit on the end of the bed. "I'm sorry," I offer.

She brings her hand to her neck. She's wearing a dressing

gown, which shields her nakedness from me, but I can still imagine every curve of her body. The little mole she has on her left shoulder, and the heaviness of her breasts in my hands.

"Will you tell me about your past?" she asks, and I'm initially confused with her meaning.

"I don't understand? What do you want to know?"

"You've been locked away for most of your life, but I don't believe that was your first time. You had too much experience and knowledge of what you like in order to get off." Tamara doesn't look at me when she speaks. Instead, she seems to have found a space on my bedroom floor that's riveting.

"Oh!" I exclaim and find my own interesting spot to look at on the old-fashioned rug, covering the wooden floor. "No, that wasn't my first time. I know it wasn't yours." She quickly looks up at me with her eyes wide open. "I mean...I...Damn. I overhead you and Victoria talking on the phone once. I didn't mean anything bad by it."

"Just you knew I was a sure thing because I'm not a virgin."

I raise an eyebrow at her, and a small smile crosses her lips as if to say she's messing with me. It dispels some of the tension in the room, and leaning back, I settle into my pillow.

"My father decided when I turned sixteen that I needed to experience a woman. Nicholas wasn't exactly a saint at eighteen and was already renowned for his appreciation of the feminine form. I think he thought maybe it would make me less strange if I lost my virginity. You know, it might cure me type of thing."

Tamara rolls her eyes but doesn't say anything.

"He had this girl brought to the house. She came into my room, lowered her robe, and was naked underneath. It was really awkward because I hadn't been prepared, and suddenly

I've got a naked woman in my bedroom. I was more interested in the differences in her form to mine than anything else. Needless to say, my father wasn't impressed. I suspect he was listening outside the door."

I go quiet and allow the memories of that day to return.

"He came into the room and showed me what to do."

"Showed you what to do?" Tamara screws her nose up in disgust at the meaning behind my statement.

"He led the girl to the bed. Explained what her breasts and pussy were before flipping her over and spreading her bum cheeks to show me her asshole. Then he lowered his trousers and proceeded to show me how to put a dick in each of those places, plus her mouth, in order to get myself off. I always remember her scream of pain when he pushed into her ass dry."

Tamara shifts closer to me on the bed. Her eyes are filled with watery tears.

"He did that? In front of you? Did the woman not protest?"

I shake my head. "She was paid to take whatever we gave to her. My father would have paid her a good amount, so she had no choice but to accept it. As for me, it was the way of the world I grew up in…silence for long periods, then my father would think of a magical way to cure his son, and I'd be thrown into some strange new situation."

"Strange new situation!" Tamara slams her fist into the bed. "This was abuse! It shouldn't have been allowed. Not just to the woman but to you as well. What type of father near enough rapes a woman in front of his sixteen-year-old son to teach him about sex?"

I can't help but let out a wry chuckle, seeing her anger at the injustice of the situation I'd found myself in. To her, it's abhorrent, but to me, it was normal.

"What happened after your father had finished with the girl?"

"I don't think I should talk about this anymore." I can no longer look at the woman seated mere millimeters away from me on the bed.

"I have to know...please."

"Tamara."

"I have to hear it from you. I need to know why I have a bruise forming around my neck. It's the only way I can understand what happened in my bedroom. I know I agreed to everything, but there's a part of me that's scared, not only because of what you did to me but also because it resulted in the best orgasm I've ever had."

"What!" I exclaim and jerk her toward me. I pull the dressing gown away from where it's tightly wrapped around her neck. "It excited you? The monster I am?"

"It excited and scared me at the same time. Please, I need to know everything. I have to understand. At the moment, I'm terrified of what it means for both of us."

My breath catches at her words, and I get the overwhelming urge to put some distance between us. I slide from the bed, despite being still naked underneath the covers, and reach for a pair of jogging bottoms, which are neatly folded on a chair in the corner of the room. I hear Tamara gasp behind me when she sees my state of undress. At the last moment, I turn to face her, so she can see my dick standing at half-mast with the need for her body. She looks down at the bed as I pull my jogging bottoms all the way up.

"I have to understand," she repeats, and I take a seat on the chair.

"My father finished himself inside her ass. When he pulled out the girl screamed, again, and I remember seeing the blood mixed with my father's semen leaking from her. He'd been uncaring with her. She was nothing more than a set of holes to abuse. It felt wrong to me, but I knew nothing better. I'd never had a positive feminine role model in my life. My nanny was ordered about by my father and shown little respect. It wasn't until I had access to the internet and television that I realized men should respect women and not abuse them. Somehow though, the darkness has stayed within me from that first encounter."

Leaning back into the chair, I allow the story of my downfall to tumble from my lips. I'm unable to look at Tamara as I speak. That fascinating spot on the floor is back, occupying my ardent stare.

"My father put himself away and pushed me toward the woman. She lay back on the bed and parted her legs. I'd seen a pussy before because Nicholas had a thing for porn magazines, and he'd bought me some. I was more interested in the anatomy of that particular part of a woman than anything else. It was interesting to see a real-life vagina in front of me. She was shaven bare, so I was able to see everything. I stood in front of her and pulled her outer lips apart to see the sensitive flesh inside. It was glistening, and I knew in some way what my father had done to her, she found it enjoyable. She'd liked being taken roughly, despite the pain that must have surged through her body. She beckoned me with her finger, and I lowered my underwear. My dick was already hard, having been turned on by the situation. Pushing myself bare inside of her, I remember it feeling soft and wet. Welcoming. After a few tentative thrusts, my father came over to me and started screaming at me, accusing me of showing my innocence, telling me the woman wanted me to fuck her like the man I should be and not the imbecile my mother had spawned.

Something inside me snapped, and I just remember my hips bucking wildly. I was only sixteen, but I was strong. I took from the woman without care while she accepted everything. I don't know why, but at the end I placed my hands around her neck and squeezed. She screamed out in orgasm, and it took me over the edge. When I came down, she wasn't breathing. I'd choked her so hard I'd completely cut off her breathing. Everything after that was such a blur. The woman was revived and paid off, but it was my father's laugh that haunts me to this day. It was evil, and it was the only time he addressed me as his son. 'Like father like son' were his exact words. I'd made him proud."

The room falls silent, neither Tamara or I speak again for a good few minutes. Both of us are trying to take in everything that has just been said. I'm sick, twisted, and freaky. She needs to run from me, right now, before I crush her under the weight of who and what I truly am.

CHAPTER EIGHT

TAMARA

I knew what had happened to him was dark, but I'd not expected something like this. His first sexual encounter had shaped him into the man I'd allowed between my thighs no more than an hour ago.

"Your father was a bad man." I finally speak, the words quivering on my lips.

"I know. I saw much more than anyone realizes." He looks toward his bedroom wall, indicating to where I already know passages reside, hidden behind the ornately decorated walls of the hall. "I kept to the shadows. I wanted to see if I really was a monster, or if what my father taught me to do was normal.

One night, when I knew Nicholas had a woman with him, I watched them together, adding voyeur to my palette of skills when it comes to sexual matters. He had the woman tied up and was taking her hard. She screamed for more, so he pulled out and used a flogger to beat her. I thought it was normal. I didn't understand about BDSM and the experimental nature of my brother's encounter. I just presumed that in order to get off, I needed to stop the girl from breathing or beat her, and so it became my norm. I wanted to warn you properly, but I lost my mind. You intoxicated me with your beauty, and I'm sorry."

"William, please." I slide from the bed. I'm confused. I'm listening to a man tell me he's been programmed to beat a woman to enjoy sex. His father really did a number on him. The man hated his son so much, and knowing William's autistic tendencies would make him susceptible to the depravation, the former Duke rejoiced. I'd studied a case at university relating to a murderer who was on the autism spectrum. He'd been taught it was normal to kill, and his brain couldn't distinguish between right and wrong because of his learned behavior. He struggled with the concept that taking another life was wrong because it was routine to him. The victim had annoyed him, and murder was the automatic response he'd learned from his father. The man had been found not guilty, in the end, on the grounds of reduced capacity but was indefinitely detained for his and the public's safety. It's different from the sexual behaviors the Duke subjected William to, but fundamentally, the principle is the same. William was taught it was right to abuse women during sex. He only realized it was wrong when he became aware of how people from the outside world treated the opposite sex, but by then it was too late. There is a darkness in William, and I don't know if I'll ever be able to rid him of it, but he excites me, and I want to get to know him better even if I'm playing with fire.

"William." I kneel before him and place my hands on his thighs. He still can't look at me, but I know this is not simply about guilt, it is also related to his autism, so I don't push him. The stimulations he's experienced today must be leaving him in a whirlwind of emotions, and I don't want to heighten his senses further. I just need him to know I understand. "I need you to listen to me."

"Ok."

"Hold your hands out."

"What?" I'm watching him and see a line of confusion mark his forehead while he still keeps his eyes focused elsewhere.

"Hold your hands out for me."

Lifting them up slowly, his fists are tightly clenched, showing the white of his knuckles, which protrude from his shaking hands.

"Open your hands." I tell him. At first, he doesn't move, so I bring my hands up and rest them on the top of his. "Please."

Gradually, he opens them but continues to hold them rigid, guarding against the demons his brain is fighting at the moment.

"Shake your hands."

"Tamara..." he starts to protest, and I begin to shake my own hands floppily above his.

"Please," I almost whisper, pulling my hands back, so I can see his. They remain still for another minute before he gradually starts to shake them. I move my arms out to my side, shaking my hands again before I take the movement up to my arms and shoulders. "Now your arms."

He stops briefly and then starts to shake his arms around. I get to my feet.

"You know what's next?" I question.

He pushes up off his chair. "I'm guessing this." William shakes his legs, and I giggle.

"Feet, toes, arms, legs, hips, head." I shake every part of my body. "Loosen up everything. Take away the stress and the worry."

"And look like a complete dork while doing it."

"Not at all."

I take William's hands in mine, and he allows me to shake him while we dance all around the room. We must do our crazy little jig for a couple of minutes before I get short of breath and stop. William's eyes meet mine for the first time since our first kiss – I can see the sorrow and fear in them. They flick down to my chest, and when I look down, I realize my dressing gown has come loose, and the bra I'm wearing underneath is showing. Though his eyes lift back to mine with lust, the trepidation still remains. I go to speak, but nothing comes out at first until a melody I've not heard in a long time enters my head and flows out from my mouth.

"Hush, little baby, don't say a word,
Mama's going to buy you a mocking bird."

William gasps.

"My mother."

I stop singing, realizing instantly what he's trying to say.

"She sang it to me as a baby. It was the only song that calmed me." He brings his hand up to the bridge of my nose and allows the tip of his finger to run down it.

*"And if that mockingbird don't sing,
Mama's going to buy you a diamond ring."*

"My mother sang it to me when I couldn't sleep." I tell him as the memory of my mother lying on the bed beside me, singing softly, comes to the forefront of my mind. We didn't have much when I was growing up, just a small room in the attic of the Viscount's house, but it was all I wanted. I had a mother who loved me, and there was no need for an absent father who never cared about me.

"I've not heard it since she sang it the day they took me from her. She was desperate to calm me down. Will you sing it to me when I need you to?"

"Always. You only have to ask."

William leans forward, and before I have a chance to think, his lips are pressed against mine. His warmth floods through my body, settling the nerves I was feeling, and dissipating the burning sensation of the raw skin on my wrists and neck. I forgive him because I know it's not his fault. The demons he's hiding within him will always surface, but there is a trust between us, which gives me hope. I push my body in closer to him and feel his hardness against my hip.

"Take me again." I say to him, pulling back from our kiss and breathing the words of my desperation into his mouth. He catches them with another kiss and leads us toward his bed. My dressing gown is pushed open, and his hands are on my breasts, cupping the flesh over my gossamer bra. I need rid of my clothes. My skin is sensitive – it feels like I need to climb out of it just to get relief.

"Please," I wantonly whimper, and William removes my dressing gown from me. Then lowering my bra, he pulls a nipple into his mouth and teases it. I'm writhing under him.

Wanting...needing...hoping. Then our eyes meet, and I see terror there in William's – it damn near rips my heart in two. I push him away when he goes to trail a path of kisses lower down my body.

"Stop," I tell him, and he regards me in confusion.

"What's wrong?"

I sit up on the bed and wrap my dressing gown around myself. William sits next to me.

"You believe you're a monster."

"Tamara, please."

"You have to believe it's not true. Tell me what was going on in your head. What made you look so scared?"

"I can't."

"Please. Trust me."

He goes silent, and I see a lone tear tumble down his cheek.

"I'll kill you," he finally says.

"What?"

"I'll forget one day how to be good and will kill you."

The words slam into my chest like a ton of bricks. I can barely breathe at his revelation because from his perspective, he believes it's the truth. He can't see the good man he truly is. This is no way to start a relationship, no matter the attraction between us.

"You can't do this, can you? Sex with me again?" I ask, and he shakes his head.

"I'm sorry. I thought I could. You were singing the song to me that my mother used to. It was beautiful, but I think I need you as a friend more than I do a lover. I've barely been free for more than a few months, and everything is alien to me. I've never been out to a fast food joint, or been to a club, a pub, or the cinema. Even cars scare the life out of me. All of my knowledge has been learned via television and books. I'm far from normal, and I fear I never will be. I need to find out what this world is about, first. I have to rid it of my father's evil, help Nicholas establish his place as the leader of the Oakfield Society, and bring the family name into the fresh, pure daylight of a new dawn. I have to repay my brother for all he's done to help me over the years, and I owe it to Victoria as well. She suffered because Nicholas was protecting me to the point he was torn in two directions, trying to save us both. I'm too consumed by these four walls and the horrors that have occurred within them, at the moment. Starting a relationship with me would only destroy you, and I don't know if I could have another person's suffering on my conscience. I'm sorry. As you can see, my dick wants you so badly I don't think he's ever going to go back down, but my brain, however fucking mis-wired it is, tells me I need to venture out and discover the world first."

I wipe away the tears that have started falling down my cheeks while William was speaking. They are not tears of remorse at being rejected by him but ones of pride for his bravery.

"Too much, too soon." I look around the room. "I can't begin to imagine what it was like being confined within this small space and the room next door for so long. I don't know what the future holds, but when this is over with the society if you still want me as a physical companion, just let me know. Until then, we are friends, and I'll help you, Nicholas, and Victoria in any way I can. You have demons you need to slay, and I'll be there to fight them with you, should you want me at your side. All you have to do is ask."

I slide from the bed and leaning forward, I press a chaste kiss to William's cheek.

"Just remember this William Cavendish, Earl of Lullington...you saved my best friend...you saved your brother...and you fought the devil who imprisoned and tortured you for most of your life...and you won. You beat the demon on the outside, now, all you have to do is slay the ones in your mind, and free yourself forever."

I pull my dressing gown all the way around me and leave William alone with his thoughts. Today has been emotional, to say the least. My body sags with exhaustion the second I get back to my room. Thoughts of my mother's betrayal, Victoria's pregnancy, Viscount Hamilton's continued denial of his part in his daughter's treatment, and the fight continuously raging inside William's head, all run through my mind. However, one thought lingers in my head as I shut my eyes to sleep – Father. Nicholas will be a father soon, William's father mistreated him badly, Victoria's nearly destroyed her, but I've never known my father and maybe it's time I tried to find out who he is...

CHAPTER NINE

WILLIAM

"I can't believe I'm returning a painting to an art gallery. This just feels so strange." Nicholas flicks a switch on a technical gadget he's holding, and all the alarms in the National Gallery in London are switched off. His little piece of wizardry was given to him by Matthew Carter and Ryan North, both MI5 alumni. I'm still amazed my brother was able to get them on side with his plan, but it seems righting wrongs is close to their hearts. We're both dressed head to toe in black with night vision goggles over our eyes. I'm liking the darkness – it's a big improvement on the flashing lights I saw, traveling into London. How anyone can sleep in this city when it's lit up like a Christmas tree almost twenty-four hours a day is beyond me.

"I think it just proves Victoria has you by the balls." I chuckle at my brother, which earns me a thump on the back. "Hey watch it! Precious cargo in hand. You don't want me to drop this fifty-million-dollar picture, now, do you?"

"Don't remind me of the value," Nicholas growls between gritted teeth. "If I didn't love my wife so much, I'd be selling this picture on the black market and using the money to wipe out all our enemies. Instead, I'm giving back one of my favorite paintings."

I hold in my hands an original work of art called 'Poppies' by Van Gogh. Nicholas stole it from the Mohamed Mahmoud Kahlil Museum in Cairo eight years ago. It's small, little more than twenty-five inches by twenty-one inches, but it's hung in Oakfield's main hall since the night Nicholas brought it home. My father was proud of him that night. The irony isn't lost on me. He's proud of me when I almost kill a woman, and of Nicholas when he steals a famous painting. Why couldn't he have been like other fathers and been proud of us for cutting our first tooth or saying our first words? No, it could only be when we committed some despicable crime.

"At least she didn't make me take it back to Cairo. British museums are so much easier to get in and out of." Nicholas takes the painting from me and places it underneath Van Gogh's self-portrait.

"Why didn't she want it back in Cairo?" I question.

"As much as she hates the painting because of the reminder of what it represents, I think she secretly wants to be able to come and see it when she can." Nicholas strips off the protective film from the painting. He's wearing special gloves, which won't leave any traces of a fingerprint.

"Makes sense. You think Cairo will allow it to stay here?"

"Not up to me. That's for them to fight out amongst themselves. I think the UK might have a bit more sway when it comes to these things, so I'm hoping so." Nicholas steps back and looks at the picture in its temporary home. "Time 'til the guard comes around?" he asks me, and I look at my watch, which I'd synchronized with the guard's timings earlier. "Five minutes and twenty-six seconds."

"Good. Plenty of time. Flick the switch on your glasses and check for fingerprints or DNA."

I do as he asks, and using a special filter, I can see the picture is clean.

"All good."

"Ok, let's get out of here. I've got a wife waiting to reward me for being a good husband."

"Didn't need to know that, Brother."

Nicholas laughs, and we leave the museum the same way we entered, via the roof. Nicholas flicks another switch on his superhero gadget, and the alarms are reset.

"The guard is going to get a big shock in about three minutes and ten seconds," I chuckle. The tension of completing the feat disappears as we make our way back to the Lexus waiting for us with my brother's driver. Throwing all the equipment in the trunk, we get in the car and remove our black clothing to reveal full dress suits below. The driver pulls away, and we are finally home free. Nicholas straightens his tie and takes out a decanter of brandy from a compartment in the car.

"Drink?" he offers.

"A small one." I tug at the neck tie, hating the fact he chose this as a disguise. We were both at a function in nearby Kensington, tonight. I hated every minute of being the sociable

Earl, but it was a necessary ruse as an essential part of our plan to return the picture. Providing us with an alibi should we be questioned. Nicholas made sure we were 'seen' even when we weren't there. I didn't ask because I'm reluctant to know the full extent of his abilities for subterfuge. My father trained him well.

I settle back in the car for the return journey to Oakfield Hall on the outskirts of the city. Shutting my eyes, I bring the amber nectar to my lips and allow it to burn down my throat with its velvety comfort.

I turn to face Nicholas who's checking his mobile with a look of worry on his face. I know instantly it's not because of our breaking and entering escapade. It's the look he gets when he's worried about his wife. "Is Victoria alright?"

"She's still feeling a little sick. Tamara prepared her a ginger tea earlier, which seemed to settle her stomach a bit."

"It must be hard seeing her feel so ill and knowing you not only caused it, but there's little you can do to help her until she's over the three-month mark."

"The consequences of not covering our dicks," my brother laments. "It's not us who suffer."

"I don't know. I think you're suffering as well. Well, you will when she gives birth. Victoria is strong, and she's going to give you hell." I can't help but laugh at my brother's impending doom. Victoria will curse him out like a sailor during labor, and if he doesn't end up with a broken hand, I'll be surprised. He's going to suffer, and then he gets to be a father and change stinky diapers. I can't help sniggering.

"I wouldn't laugh at me too much, little brother."

"Yeah, not going to happen to me." I sit back smugly and bring the brandy to my lips.

"So, the screaming I heard coming from Tamara's room had nothing to do with you?"

"What?" I spit my brandy out over the chair in front of me. "You heard? Does Victoria know? Is she going to kill me?"

"Why would she kill you?" Nicholas frowns. "She's happy. She'd love having Tamara as her sister-in-law. She's seen the attraction between you both since the moment you first met. Wouldn't surprise me if she's overly sung your praises to Tamara for matchmaking purposes."

"It won't happen," I reply bluntly. Nicholas puts his brandy down and turns to face me. I won't look at him, though. If I need to, I'll shut my eyes, so I don't have to look directly into his. My fingers are itching to tap or swipe – to start their comforting routine. Nicholas reaches over and takes the brandy from my hand. I instantly bring my hand up to my ear and swipe across it then through my hair. One, two taps on the floor with my foot, and I'm already feeling calmer, but I know Nicholas isn't going to stop his questioning.

"William, you slept with Tamara?" he questions.

"Yes."

My brother pauses, and I know he's trying to find the right words for what he wants to say next.

"Did you hurt her?"

I want to say no – to tell him she enjoyed it as much as I did because her tight little pussy milked me so much I was seeing fucking stars.

"I think so." Is the only answer I can give. My hands do their routine again.

"How did you hurt her?"

"She's got a bruised neck and rope burns on her wrists."

"Shit!" my brother exclaims. "What did she say? After? During? Did she ask you to stop?"

I think back through the entire time we were together. She pleaded and pleaded with me for more. She never once asked me to stop.

"No. She says I'm not a monster."

"She liked it rough?" my brother questions with an element of shock in his voice. He knows what I like. He's seen the girls who've left my room after I've finished with them.

"I...don't know," I stammer. I want to hide away, now. I don't want to continue this conversation. It's too confusing for me. My mind hurts... my head hurts. Too much.

We pull up the long driveway to the house, and before the car stops, I'm out and running up to my rooms. Nicholas is after me, and I pass Victoria and Tamara on the stairs. They look at me in confusion, but I don't stop – I need to get to my safe place. My sanctuary. The only place I know I can be me and won't be judged. Behind me, I hear Victoria call to Nicholas.

"Nicholas what's wrong?"

"Give me a few minutes," he replies as his footsteps follow me up the stairs.

I enter my rooms and push the door shut, but I'm not quick enough to lock it before Nicholas uses his strength to force it open. I start to pace the room, and Nicholas tries to pull me to a halt and get me to look at him, but I shove him away.

"William, listen to me. It's alright. Tamara is fine. If she didn't tell you to stop, then you did nothing wrong."

"I strangled her."

"It can be a part of sex, not all the time, but some people do like it. It doesn't mean you're like him."

We both freeze. The truth of the matter hits us both hard. It's what we both fear. Have I been so damaged that I'm just the same as our father? Nicholas feared it about himself for so long until Victoria helped him to recognize he's his own man. But I can't see that. All I see when I look in the mirror is my father's reflection staring back out at me. He created the person I am. The freak who pointed a gun at his own father's head and pulled the trigger. I killed my father, and I don't have any regrets. No, if I had the chance, I'd do it again. Only next time, I'd make it more painful.

"William?" My brother tries to reach out to touch me, but I push him away.

"You need to leave, Nicholas. Go be with your wife. Protect her and love her. Keep the darkness from consuming you. She's the key to you staying on the right side."

"Tamara could be yours," my brother immediately fires back.

"Monsters don't fall in love. They exist only to destroy. Tamara's too innocent to be allowed on my path. I'll drag her down with me to hell."

"William, you have to listen to me."

My brother attempts to grab me for a final time, but I summon all the strength I have and send him flying across the room. My mind has descended into the dark recess where my anxieties mix with the rejection I faced for so many years. I no longer see what can be, only what is. I'm a freak who should continue to be hidden away for the world's protection.

Picking up a chair, I slam it into the wall beside me. It disintegrates into little pieces of splintered wood. Next comes a chest of drawers. With inhuman strength, I send them flying. Trinkets and pictures smash on the floor.

I'm vaguely aware of Victoria running into the room. She hands something to Nicholas – the only method of subduing the overstimulation and breakdown in me. I stop and stand still waiting for the sharp prick of the hypodermic in my neck, and when it comes, the numbing drugs flow into my body. Before the darkness of a sedated sleep claims me, I look up to see Tamara, standing at the doorway. Her eyes are full of the one thing I never wanted to see in them: sorrow. Despair for what I am, and what I can be.

CHAPTER TEN

TAMARA

"I'm never getting pregnant if this is what it does to you." I hold back Victoria's hair as she dry heaves into the toilet. She's been running back and forth to the bathroom for the last half an hour, but nothing has come up. It's early in the morning, a little after five am, and I spent last night sleeping in the same bed as her. She hates to sleep alone since her ordeal, and Nicholas wanted to stay with his brother to check on him when he woke. It wasn't exactly how I imagined I'd be waking up this morning, but at least it's giving me a distraction from worrying about William. I can see he's falling apart even further, and a feeling of guilt weighs heavy within me. A fear that I'm to blame because I pushed him into having sex with me, and it made him confront a side of himself he's hidden away and managed to control for so long. Rubbing Victoria's back and whispering words of encouragement to her as she fights her morning sickness, helps me to push the culpability aside, for now.

"You'll get pregnant one day, and I'll be there reminding you of this moment." She heaves again and then sits with her back against the clawfoot bath. "I feel like shit."

I can't help but laugh at the way her face screws up. She's not looking like the elegant Duchess she likes to portray in public, at the moment.

"Hate to say it, but you look it as well," I respond, handing her a glass of water with lemon in it.

"Some friend you are." She throws the towel she's been holding at me. "I want it to stop."

"Just remember it means that there's a healthy little baby in your tummy, taking all the good stuff from its mummy and leaving her exhausted."

She snorts.

"Sounds just like Nicholas after a mammoth sex session."

I put my fingers in my ears.

"La, la, la."

"I should've done that the other night." Victoria responds and raises an eyebrow at me.

Lowering my hands, I push up onto my feet from the crouching position I was in and reach out to help her to stand.

"I don't know what you mean." I play dumb as we go back into her room, and I pass her a dressing gown to cover her pajamas.

"Oh come on, the entire household heard you when you climaxed. Damn, Tammy, you're a screamer."

"Ria." I use my nickname for her and scold her with a scowl.

"It's not a problem. I'm happy about it. Are you a couple now?"

"I don't want to talk about this," I tell her and wrap my own dressing gown around my shoulders.

"It must have been hard seeing him have a meltdown last night. I've seen it a couple of times before. Nicholas hates using the sedative, but William has hurt himself previously, and he'll do anything to prevent that."

"Ria, not now!" I snap and walk out of the room and down the stairs toward the kitchen with Victoria following close behind me. In silence, I prepare myself an americano and a ginger tea for her to settle her stomach.

"I'm sorry," she says when I hand it to her.

"So am I," I respond as I add a little milk to my coffee and stir it. "It was hard to see him like that last night. I'm worried what happened between us has made him believe things, which aren't true."

"What do you mean?" Victoria asks, taking her tea and sitting down at a little table in the corner of the vast kitchen. It's normally a hive of activity with meals being prepared for the Cavendish family, but at this early hour, it's empty.

"The sex. It was good, really good, but a little rough." I join her at the table and swirl my coffee around in the cup, hoping for it to cool quicker, so I can get some caffeine goodness in me to calm my nerves.

"How rough?"

Last night when we slept together, I made sure I wore a

high-necked top with extra-long sleeves to hide my bruises. I lower my dressing gown and roll up the sleeves of my top. Victoria's eyes go wide on seeing the red marks marring my arms. Biting my lip, I next bring my fingers up to the neck of my t-shirt and pull it down. This time she gasps.

"Tammy! What did he do?"

"I was tied to the bed, and when we orgasmed, he choked me."

"Shit!" she exclaims at the same moment the chef comes into the kitchen. I quickly let go of my t-shirt, covering the contusions around my neck once again.

"Sorry, my lady, I wasn't aware you were in here." The chef bows. "Is there something you need? Breakfast?"

"No, it's fine. We'll get out of your way. I'm sure you don't need me with my non-existent cooking skills in your kitchen."

"It's not a problem. If you and Miss Bennett need to talk, I can prepare ingredients in the pantry for now," the chef replies as he backs out toward the kitchen door.

"Thank you," Victoria tells him, and he disappears. She turns to me again, and it's all I can do to hold back the tears I've been wanting to let flow for the last twenty-four hours.

"Was it consensual? The sex…and the choking?"

"I pleaded with him to do whatever he needed to me."

"That doesn't mean it was right. Did you ask him to stop?"

"No, that's the thing," I say and finally take a sip of my coffee, which is now cool enough. "I enjoyed it. It scared the hell out of me, but it was the best orgasm I've ever had."

"Wow." Victoria stares at me with her mouth wide open.

"Can I ask you something?" I inquire hesitantly.

"You can. It's not a guarantee I'll answer, though."

"Is Nicholas rough?"

Victoria lets out a long exhale. "The thing you have to understand about the Cavendish boys is that virtually all the maternal figures in their life have been abused women. It's the norm to them. For a long time, Nicholas knew what he was doing was wrong, but the pressure he was under and the lack of maternal love meant he couldn't stop what was happening. That doesn't mean he's ever left me as bruised as William has you."

My eyes narrow at Victoria, knowing exactly what Nicholas did to her when they first met.

"Ok, yeah he branded me and led me around in a scold's bridle while his band of merry men whipped me. That's what I mean, though. No matter how much they care for a woman, it's hard for them after so many years of abuse to initially behave appropriately. Many people would say it should be instantaneous and they are monsters for not immediately protecting us, but their father's way of life is so ingrained into them they struggle to see past it. Unable to believe in a potential normality until they've worked through everything else. Their father skewed their moral compass and for all the brashness Nicholas, especially, likes to portray, underneath he's just a man trying to find his way in a fucked-up world."

"Their father really did a number on them both," I say woefully and finish my coffee while Victoria swallows the last mouthful of her tea.

"He did. Nicholas still struggles some days, but I've no worries about him being a good father despite his own father's influence. Of course, William has had to adjust to so much more. He's had to deal with his autism, and the fact he was locked away for so long, as well as coping with the violence he himself experienced and saw his father expend at every turn.

His heart is good, though. He saved me when he could have so easily treated me like the others did. He had plenty of opportunities to rape me if he'd truly been the monster he now thinks he is, but he didn't. That shows the real truth of him. He just needs some time to come to terms with all the changes around him."

"So, I've not set him back by sleeping with him."

"No. You've given him food for thought."

"I hope so." I reach forward and squeeze her hand.

"Thanks, Ria."

"You're my best friend. I'm always going to help you."

Victoria winks at me and gets to her feet. "Speaking of food for thought, I had an idea in the night and wanted to run it by your legal brain. Come with me."

I follow my best friend as she meanders through the seemingly endless corridors of Oakfield Hall. It's lovely to see her in her element as the mistress of this place. It must be hard for her to love the building after all the history the four walls have seen, but somehow, she seems to soften the harsh exterior. She finally stops in front of a door marked as the 'Duke's Office'. She pushes it open, and I see two desks facing each other in the middle of the room. The one to the left of me has a pile of papers with a half-empty brandy glass placed on top. It's the more masculine of the two desks. The other one has a white folder covered in roses on it as well as a small vase with a single, fresh red rose. This is obviously Victoria's desk. Nobody else would have rose stationery. She's obsessed with the flower. Picking up the folder, she flicks through it.

"Nicholas has managed to get most of the members of the society to sign up to the new rules. Many of them were thankful for the change. Abusing women didn't sit well with them. However, a few have been a bit more hesitant. Nicholas has barred them from all meetings, but he's been following their actions closely, and it looks like they are going to try to start causing trouble. We could have all the assets they want to use frozen by illegal means, but that gives them fuel against us. We want to try to do everything as legally as possible, and that is where you come in." Victoria pauses and hands me a piece of paper. "Can you figure out a legal way to suspend any funds these people have?"

I look down at the list. It consists of a few names, but two stand out to me, in particular. Lord West and Viscount Hamilton. I know Lord West from stories about one of the girls who disappeared, and Viscount Hamilton is Victoria's father, of course.

"You want me to go against your father?" I look up from the list to Victoria.

"I don't think we have a choice," she says matter of factly, but I can tell it's hurting her. He's still her father, no matter what he did to her. She does have some good memories of him being a caring parent toward her. In fact, we both do while growing up together.

"This could harm Theo in the end."

"I know. When Nicholas eventually allows me to visit my father's estate, I want to try and talk to my brother. See if I can explain to him everything that's happened."

"It might not be that easy."

"We have to do this, Tamara. We have to put a stop to what they are doing. Not just for the sake of the women involved, but for Nicholas and William too. They're out from under their father's shadow and can finally be their own men, but if my father has his way, he'll destroy them, so he can hold all the power and be able to do whatever he wants with women, again. I know his true colors now."

I look down at the names on the paper and back up to my friend. Ideas start to form in my head about what can be done to ruin the names and freeze the assets of these powerful, evil men.

"I'll do it."

CHAPTER ELEVEN

WILLIAM

"*William. You awake?*" The deep timbre of a masculine voice draws me from my slumber, and I open my eyes. Looking over to my alarm clock, it tells me it's the early hours of the morning.

"Nicholas?" I question.

"No, it's me," the voice replies, and in my sleep induced haze, I have to open my eyes to see who's in my room. When I open them, I see my friend Lord West, and he's accompanied by a vivacious blonde who's waving enthusiastically at me.

"Hello." I sit up, rubbing my eyes and yawning. "What's going on?"

"I've brought you a present." West leers at me and pushes the girl on his arm forward.

"It's not really the sort of present I want at three am. I'd rather another couple of hours sleep." I grunt and slide back down in the bed.

"Jesus, William. You really are strange. If I was to bring a willing woman to most blokes, they'd get their dick out and say, 'which hole is mine?'. But you would rather sleep."

"Fuck you, West," I retort. "If she wants my dick, she can get it out and bounce on it."

My friend laughs. "You heard him, love. Time to go all cowboy on his dick."

"That's not something you have to ask me to do twice, not if he's as good with it as you are," the woman sing-songs, and I try to ignore them even though I know it will be futile.

"He's not as good as me, babe, but he knows what to do with it. He's learned from the master after all. He's the Duke's son."

"Nicholas?" she exclaims.

"No, William," West replies, and I can hear them getting nearer to the bed.

"But I didn't think anyone ever saw him. There are rumors he's disfigured and can't speak because he's got the brain of a baby."

"Well, you've heard him speak, so I think that dispels that theory." Before I have a chance to grab the sheets, my friend pulls them off leaving me naked in front of him and the girl.

"Fucking hell, West!" I try to grab them back from him, but he's thrown them across the room, and the girl is crawling up the bed toward me before I have a chance to do anything about it.

"I don't see any disfigurements either. Why does the Duke hide him away?" She stares at me as she speaks, cocking her head from side to side as if she's examining me. I shut my eyes to try and block it all out while my hands go to my junk to cover it, so I'm not on display for them both.

"He's got something called autism. His brain is wired funny, or some shit like that. The Duke says he acts strange in polite society, and he's worried about him embarrassing him, so it's best to keep him hidden away."

"That's a shame," the girl laments woefully. "He's pretty handsome. He'd be a catch in our circles."

"The Duke allows you in here to play, but William's not allowed out."

The girl giggles, sending an eerie shiver down my spine.

"As long as I get to play, that's all I want."

"You do realize I'm lying here, trying to sleep," I snap.

"Babe, suck his dick. We need to wake him up a bit more."

I hold on tighter to my junk, but it's to no avail. The woman slides herself over my body, tasting it as she works her way down to where my traitorous dick hardens. I let go of it, and she wraps her mouth around the length, causing it to stiffen further. By the time she finishes licking up the sides of my shaft and sucking on my balls, I'm hard enough to pound nails. I push her off before she makes me come because there's no point in wasting an orgasm if it's going to be unsatisfactory. No, I need more stimulation to persuade me to give up my cum. West comes behind her, and I can see him removing her clothes. He's giving me a display, knowing that this is the way we work best together. He lets me watch as he unwraps the present and takes her first before giving me what is left to fuck into complete oblivion. His clothes fall to the floor as he orders her to lie down on the bed, and I slide over to the side, so she has enough room to get on. Her hand reaches out for my dick, and she pumps it a few times before I grab her wrist and stop it. I don't need to tell her – the tight grip of my fingers around her delicate skin is enough. As she's one of West's girls, she'll be trained for what is about to happen to her. He wouldn't use her if she wasn't. I'm too dangerous to be left with a novice in our dark world. My father decreed, after the events surrounding the loss of my virginity, that he didn't want to have to deal with any dead bodies covered in my DNA. It would be too much of an inconvenience for him, especially when he's got better things to do like fuck his own slut into a hospital or worse.

"Here's what's going to happen," West tells the girl who's still holding my dick but no longer moving her hand. She turns her attention to the other man in the room. "I'm in the mood for something a little different tonight. Something daring. Something dark," West announces.

"Sounds exciting," the girl purrs, and I take a moment to examine her body. She's not what I'd call pretty although I'm sure most people would. She's too thin with not enough to grab hold of except for her chest, which is more than a handful, but I'm fairly certain they're not real. Her hair is a brilliant blonde, and with a face full of make-up there's nothing natural about her. Even her protruding ribs are fake – the result of her starving herself to give her appearance the catwalk look. I push her hand off my dick and shift so I'm standing. I take my own dick in hand, giving it a couple of hard pumps just to take the edge off the tension I feel building in my balls. I may not find this woman sexy, but what is about to happen will be all I need to get me off, when the time is right.

"It's very exciting." West says, drawing my attention back to him as he pulls a small knife from his pocket. "It's been a while since you've bled for me, beautiful. I think it's about time we painted the bed crimson, don't you?"

"Yes, please," the woman hisses with excitement, and I have to wonder about the mentality of someone who'd let a man do this to her. She must trust West implicitly not to harm her. I wouldn't trust him as far as I could throw him, but then I've seen some of the things this man has done to women. I'll never forget the night I heard pained screaming coming from my father's room. I used the secret passageway to investigate what was happening. My father and West were sharing a girl with one in her ass and the other in her pussy. She was covered in blood and bruises where they'd obviously beaten her. She was crying and pleading for them to stop, but neither did. They continued to assault her for the next few hours before West put a gun to her head and blew her brains out. I may lose myself during the moment, but I would never deliberately do that to a woman. She has to consent to what I do, and even though sending that poor girl to heaven may have been a blessing, it's not something I could ever do. Maybe that's why I'm the monster. I don't have the guts to finish the job properly and put them out of their misery after I've destroyed them.

"Hey, William. You going to concentrate on the job in hand, or are you just going to stand there and play with your dick like the pussy you are." West brings me out of my reflection with his harsh words, and I watch as he swirls his tongue around a line of blood on the girl's breast.

"So good," she moans, and he flicks the knife over her other tit. The crimson essence floods to the surface and trickles down over her nipple. "You want some?" the girl asks me, and I shake my head. Blood play is West's thing, not mine. I just need a hole to stick my dick in at the end.

"I'll watch, for now."

West takes his knife lower, making a few small cuts on the girl's stomach as he goes. When he gets to her pussy, he pulls the folds apart and swipes the knife over the delicate flesh. The girl screams in pain this time, not pleasure.

"Fuck, that hurt." She tries to shut her legs, but West pulls them apart and licks the length of her slit. He has blood round his mouth when he brings his head back up. "Don't do that again," the girl demands, but West doesn't listen to her. He cuts the other side of her *folds, and I know in that instant this has turned darker and into something the girl wasn't expecting.*

"My cunt. I'll treat it the way I want. William, stick your dick in her mouth to shut her up," West orders, but I'm going nowhere near the girl who's now trying to escape from the clutches of my friend.

"Fuck off. She'll bite it."

"Well, hold her down, so I can rip her pussy in two." He momentarily let's go of the struggling feminine form and gets a whack to the face from her fist. He retaliates with his own, and I hear the crunch of the girl's nose as it breaks. West flips her over and puts his whole weight on her. "Now, William, or do I need to tell your father you're being a freak again. He'll send you away this time – remember what he said about being sick of you showing him up. He'll make sure you never see Nicholas again."

Those final few words have me releasing my deflated cock and using my strength to hold the girl down, so she can't struggle anymore. West pulls her ass up and without warning slides hard into her pussy as she screams out in pain, and I switch off. My mind goes to its place of serenity, and I don't hear the cries or the pleas any longer. I'll suffer later for treating my brain this way. I know I'll meltdown, but for now I feel safe.

The gun going off brings me out of heaven. Blood splatters all over me, and the girl I'd been holding becomes a dead weight in my arms.

"Fucking cunt!" West exclaims, and I step backward. My hand goes to my nose and swipes across it, no doubt smearing blood and other matter across my face. "Bitch got herself pregnant. I'm not going to have some piece of trash like her lauding that over me for the rest of my life. Shame, she had a fucking magical pussy. Why don't you try it? I know you like them barely breathing. She'll still be nice and wet down there. I tore her up a bit. Lots of blood to ease the flow."

I look down to his dick and see it's covered in blood.

"Get out." I feel my fists forming into balls. West just laughs.

"Oh, come on, William. Stop being a freak. You losing your hard-on isn't my fault. It's all that wrong wiring in your brain." The laugh he expels is eerie, almost demonic in nature. People call me a freak, but the man in front of me has just fucked a woman and shot her in the head. In my fucking bed! "I best go tell your daddy about our little accident, hadn't I? Do us a favor, get your dick wet as well. Makes you look more culpable."

It's then I realize this has been a ruse all along. It's easier for my father to clear this mess up than it would be for West to do it himself. My father won't have our name dragged through the mud, so he'll get rid of the body without consequence for West or for me. Believing I'm the freak – the dangerous, dark monster who is capable of such atrocities. West leaves the room, and I'm alone with the dead girl. The way she's fallen, I can see her pussy on display covered in blood mixed with West's cum. I could do what they expect from me but I won't. I'm not that sort of person.

"William?" My brother's voice penetrates the foggy haze of my brain. "William, talk to me please?"

"Nicholas? What happened?"

"You had a meltdown. Victoria and I injected you with the sedative to calm you down. I didn't want to do it, but I was so afraid you'd hurt yourself."

I slowly open my eyes and allow my vision to acclimatize to where I am, which turns out to be my bedroom, and on my bed. I flinch, half expecting the bed to be covered in blood and with the body of a dead girl from what, I now realize. was a nightmare based on my memories.

"William?" Nicholas reaches out to touch me and ground me.

"I was back there."

"Back where?" he questions with confusion etched on his brow.

"The night West murdered the girl in my bed."

Nicholas exhales deeply and shuts his eyes.

"You did the right thing that night. You came and found me. Our father checked the DNA. There was none of yours inside her, only West's. It was all him. Not you."

"But…" I try to argue with him, but with an authoritative wave of his hand, he silences me.

"You've been too overstimulated the last few days. You need to rest. These memories are of a time in the past. Lord West will never have access to this house again, and you're nothing like the monster he is. When I can finally bring him down, then another piece of the corrupt society our father kept will fall. William, you're my brother. I love you dearly, and I will protect you always. Don't fear the world. Embrace it and allow it to give you the life you deserve."

My brother gets to his feet and straightens out his trousers. I can tell from the creases he's been sitting by my bed for several hours.

"I'm going to check on Victoria, but I'll be back up with some food. I'm the Duke, now, and I'm ordering you to rest for a few days. Away from that crazy outside world full of lights and sounds. God knows it drives me insane, most of the time. We'll spend time just the four of us, trying to figure out how to get rid of West and Viscount Hamilton, so we can live our lives freely."

My brother leaves the room, and I'm left alone in the silence, once again. I want to shut my eyes and sleep for longer, but I'm scared. I know I didn't touch that girl the night she died, but I'm terrified if I fall asleep, the conclusion to the nightmare might change.

CHAPTER TWELVE

TAMARA

The words on the computer screen in front of me are starting to go blurry, I've been staring at them for so long. Line after line of contract law. During my time training, I'd learned a bit about each division of the law: statute, criminal, common, and civil, but it would've blown my mind to delve too deeply into all of them. So, when it had been time to specialize, I'd gone down the criminal law route. Little did I know it would come in handy in the future because my best friend was going to marry into a notoriously criminal society. My head hurts, and my hands are jittery from all the coffee I've been drinking, but I need to continue reading to see if there is any legal way of dissolving the society as it was, and leaving those opposed to Nicholas' new rule financially ruined. Along with help from associates of Nicholas, I've applied for the assets to be frozen of two of the main culprits who refuse to toe the line: Lord West and Viscount Hamilton. I don't expect that to stick for long, though. The police must have thought me insane when I presented them with some bullshit about them funding terrorists.

After I read the same paragraph for what must be the sixth time, I know I need to take a break, and I stand up from the desk I'm using in Nicholas' office. The office was big enough for two extra desks, matching his and Victoria's, to be brought in, and there is still sufficient space to perform a 'jig' if you are so inclined– I'm not. But maybe just a stretch or two. I arch my back, and bringing my arms up above my head, I stretch them before lowering them and shaking out my legs. Yawning, I debate getting another coffee, but I know I'll never sleep if I have any more caffeine. I'll be dancing off the ceiling. No, the best thing I can do is to call it a night, but something is drawing me back to the computer.

A couple of months ago, I took one of those swab DNA tests for the ancestry website everyone raved about. A friend of mine had done it at university and found out an old family tale about her having Indian blood was true, and in fact a quarter of her DNA originated from that continent. She was thrilled to have it confirmed. I already know from my mother's side that my ancestry is African via my grandfather, who came to this country after World War One, and Anglo Saxon from my grandmother, whose family originated from Suffolk. By doing the test, I was really hoping to see if I could link into any relatives on my father's side, which might give me an idea of who he is. My mother has never told me the story of my birth. It's something I've always wondered about, but I can't force her to tell me. Something happened to her, and I'm scared to find out what it was, but I need to know where I come from, and this is my only means, at the moment, to try and discover more.

I shut my eyes and take a deep breath. I had notification a few weeks ago the results were back, but I've been too scared to look at them. Opening my eyes, I flick my mouse to bring up a new browser page and type in the website address. I log into my account and open up the tab labelled DNA, which instantly brings up my results. Twenty-five percent African, I expected that. I scroll further down, and my eyes flick over the rest of my genetic make-up.

"Tamara, what are you still doing up? It's past midnight." William strolls into the room. His eyes move to the computer screen and then up to me. I know I must have a guilty look on my face because his brows frown in the center. "What are you doing?"

"Nothing." I try to hide the tremble in my voice, but I know I fail.

"Tamara. Step away from the screen."

"It's nothing."

He raises an eyebrow at me, and then walking up to me, he lifts me up in the air. I bring the wireless mouse with me because my grip is so tight on it.

"DNA results, I did this once. I wanted to try and prove I wasn't linked to my father. It didn't work." He shrugs and looks down. "Mmm...let me see, totally British apart from your grandfather."

I nod, not able to form words. My heart is beating so fast. I've not even told Victoria I'm doing this. I know she wanted to do it at one time, but her father wouldn't let her. I think she got Theodore to do it, instead, but I'm not sure.

"You've got a lot of Scottish in there as well. Wonder where from? Probably your father."

William halts his train of thought.

"Shit. Sorry. I didn't mean..."

"It's ok."

I scramble back to the computer and close the browser page.

"Wait, did you check your matches? It could give you an idea about who your father is."

"No. William, please."

He reaches out, takes the mouse from my hand, and lays it down on the table. Then placing his hand on top of the laptop, he shuts it down.

"Come with me."

He holds out his hand. I look at it and back up at him, debating on whether to take it or not. I'm freaking out. I've just learned whoever my father is/was is most probably British. That's more than I've known all my life. I need comfort, but the last time I took William's hand, it led to him becoming so overstimulated that he broke down and near enough destroyed his room. I can't let that happen again.

"I'm ok." I keep my hands by my side.

"Ok." He looks defeated and lowers his head. "I wasn't going to..." Stopping, he turns away, and walks over to a cabinet in the corner of the room. He opens a drawer, pulls out a hip flask, and comes back over to me. "You had a shock. I was going to get you a drink. That's all. I understand completely that you want to know where you come from. They say autism is hereditary, normally down the male line. I would love to know if my past ancestors had it. Maybe find out more about what makes me who I am."

He unscrews the hip flask and gives it to me before turning and going back to the door.

"William," I call out, guilt washing over me because he thinks I'm refusing to go with him in case he hurts me when in reality, I'm the one who's inflicting the pain.

"You should get some sleep, it's late. If you get too tired, you'll be no good at reading through all that law stuff," William replies.

He doesn't turn back to face me but leaves the room with his hand flicking around his head. I look back at the computer. The answers to everything lie within it somewhere, but right now, I just need to sleep.

CHAPTER THIRTEEN

WILLIAM

Turning over in my bed, I reach out for my phone, and through bleary eyes, I look at the time. Ten am. Urgh! I was supposed to help Nicholas in a meeting at nine. I guess he chose not to wake me. I should be grateful for small mercies since it was past two before I fell asleep. After speaking to Tamara, I needed something to clear my mind of the thoughts of failure, which I had running through it. It was then I remembered the app Nicholas had discovered and installed on my phone. A flag quiz. I spent the next two hours trying to beat my best scores from the previous times I'd played it, and needless to say, I did so with ease and fell asleep at two with a contented brain. Sadly, I've not woken with one though. Having still got the vision in my head of Tamara as she refused my hand, fearing I would hurt her again. All I wanted to do was comfort her with a stiff drink, but she thought I wanted more and was scared. Scared of me. I need to stay away from her. Give her time to realize...well, there is nothing to realize – I am a monster. She just needs to know I won't hurt her. I'll use the memory I have of her sweet velvety pussy for my needs, but I won't ever abuse the real thing again.

Sliding from my bed, I pull on a pair of jogging bottoms that had been lying, discarded from a previous day, on my bedroom floor. I fumble sleepily into the bathroom, take a piss, and splash some water on my face. If I'm hiding out all day, I don't need to be clean and presentable. Going back into my bedroom, I grab a t-shirt from a drawer and pull it on over my head.

I've got two choices now. Go in search of food, which is likely to be quicker, or order something to be brought up. My brother is currently running Oakfield Hall on skeleton staff while we sort out the issues with the society. Less chance of any underhand dealings being discovered that way. But I really don't want to risk seeing Tamara, so my stomach is going to have to wait. I pick up the intercom phone and call down to the kitchen.

"My Lord, William," the chef answers in a cheerful manner.

"Morning," I try to reply with the same happiness. "I'm going to take my breakfast in my rooms today. Can you send it up, please?"

"Of course, anything in particular you'd like?"

"No, just the usual."

I don't know why the chef bothers to ask. I've eaten the

same thing, now, for twenty years. Two Weetabix with full fat milk and a teaspoon of sugar, followed by two slices of white bread toast with strawberry jam, which mustn't have any lumps in. I wash it all down with a glass of apple juice. No coffee, tea, fancy French pastries, or even sausage, bacon and eggs for me. Cereal, toast, and apple juice is all I need to start the day right.

"It could be a little while as the staff are busy with the Duke and his meeting. I'll see if I can bring it up myself." I can hear the chef start to juggle pans in the background. I know he's busy as well, and I appreciate the kind gesture.

"No hurry. I'll be in the playroom," I inform him and hang up.

Before I leave my bedroom, I push my feet into a pair of warm woolen slippers. Oakfield Hall has an abundance of wooden and marble floors, costing a small fortune to heat. It's often easier to wrap up warm in the colder months. I grab a sweater and slip it on over my head then leave my rooms and head down the corridor to the room Nicholas and I share. This place is our sanctuary, and only we're allowed in it. It's the place we came to as boys, whiling away the hours of boredom and monotony that came from being the sons of a Duke who wanted nothing to do with us until we were old enough to be useful. That happened at the age of ten for Nicholas, but it never happened for me. I was never of importance to my father. I was the spare, and a damaged one at that.

I push open the door to the room, and I'm immediately transported back to my childhood with visions of Nicholas and I running around playing cops and robbers. He was always the robber. Ironic really! When he became more involved in his duties as the future Duke, I discovered a love for Lego, and proudly displayed in the room, now, are many of the creations I made. I was obsessed with it and would sit for hours religiously following the instructions until I'd built what I was supposed to. I remember once there was a piece missing from a pack, and unable to cope with that, I started to have a meltdown. How could I complete what I was doing without that piece? I had to finish it. I'd started, and now it would remain forever incomplete. Nicholas found me sitting in a corner with my fists clenched tightly into little balls. He immediately broke apart a creation he'd made and found the piece I needed. The memory brings back happy thoughts for me, and I seek the model out in the row of my Star Wars builds. The Millennium Falcon sits proudly next to my Death Star and Sand Crawler. Like many boys, I went through a Star Wars phase. I guess, like most, I haven't really stopped. I still have regular binge-watching marathons.

Completing these three massive projects was my greatest feat in life. The instructions sit beside the Falcon, and I know instantly how my day of hiding will be spent. I pick up the Falcon and the instructions and bring them over to some cushions laid out on the floor. Placing them both down, I begin the painstaking process of pulling the Millennium Falcon apart, so I can rebuild it, once again.

After several hours and a half-eaten breakfast followed up by a half-eaten ham sandwich for lunch, I'm halfway through the rebuilding of Hans Solo's pride and joy. I'm just fixing one of the guns in place when I hear soft steps behind me. I wait a beat and turn my head around to see Tamara halfway across the room.

"Out!" I snap at her, and she flinches back but doesn't stop. "You can't be in here."

"Nicholas gave me a note to say I could come in to talk to you." Now standing in front of me, she bends down to place the note on the floor. "He said I'm forbidden to touch your Lego though."

My eyes skim over the note, and I see Nicholas has even written that exact phrase down. I can't help but snort out a laugh.

"He said something about girls not understanding the dynamics of what it takes to build these complex structures, and if I touch them, I'll break them."

I can't help but let another chuckle escape at her comment. I can picture Nicholas saying those exact words with his arms folded sternly across his chest, and his brows furrowed together. I can also picture Victoria behind him rolling her eyes in frustration at her chauvinist husband.

"I'm surprised he didn't tell you that we don't have pink and purple Lego, so you wouldn't be interested anyway."

"I think it was on the tip of his tongue, but Victoria purposely stood on his foot with her Louboutin's to shut him up before he dug an even bigger hole for himself."

"That's my brother for you!" I roll my eyes and pat the bean bag next to me for her to take a seat.

"Did you make all these?" Tamara asks as she gracefully lowers herself until she's sitting with her legs tucked under her bottom. She's wearing blue jeans and a maroon sweater today. It seems strange not to see her in the skirts and blouses she favors.

"I did...well, except for a few small bits. Nicholas was never good at following instructions."

"I can see him being that way."

"You've no idea." I crack another smile. Tamara goes quiet. "Is everything alright?" I ask her.

"Yes." She looks up at me, but I can't meet her eyes. I flick my ear then my nose. I know I'm doing it, but it's not something I can stop.

"I wanted to ask you something."

"Ok," I reply hesitantly.

"I've got this meeting in an hour, and I wondered if you would come with me? I volunteer at a daycare center whenever I can, and it'd be good for the children to meet a real-life Earl."

"I don't know." My initial thought is one of terror. Lots of people and noisy children.

"Please," Tamara almost whispers her plea, and I simply can't say no.

"Alright. I'll get ready to go."

CHAPTER FOURTEEN

TAMARA

The car pulls up outside the day care center, and I can't help but feel a little nervous. I've not told William the entire truth about this visit because I know he wouldn't have come. I just hope he's prepared to forgive me because I think he needs to see this place.

The driver opens my car door, and William comes around to my side to help me out of the car.

"If I end up with anything sticky on my clothes, you're washing it off. I don't like getting my hands dirty."

I click my tongue at him and walk off with a sway of my

hips. "You forget. I've seen you eat. That's where anything sticky on you will come from."

"Hey!" he calls indignantly after me, but I can hear the amusement in his voice. He catches up with me, and I link my arm through his offered one. "When did you start coming here?"

"I was doing a certificate at school when I was sixteen – for part of it I needed to do some voluntary work for thirty hours. The Viscount helped me to find a place here. I stayed on afterward and help out whenever I can."

"Sounds good. So, is it just like a nursery? I don't really know the term day care," William asks, holding the door open for me to walk into the reception.

"Sort of," I reply, and before he has a chance to question me further, I'm speeding toward the receptionist, a short, grey haired lady called Eve. She's been working here since before I started, and I'm sure she told me she started back in the early nineties. She doesn't get paid for her job. She does it out of the kindness of her heart. They've tried to offer her a salary on numerous occasions, but each time, she's said no.

"Tamara, I heard you were coming in. Fantastic to see you." The spirited lady, who's age I'd guess is in the late fifties, jumps to her feet and comes around the reception desk to greet me with a big hug. "Congratulations. I hear you're qualified now. We're all so proud of you. You worked so hard. I bet you've already got a job lined up at one of those prestigious London firms."

I can't help but laugh at her excitement over the fact I'm now a qualified lawyer. "I've got a place at one, yes. I've still not decided if I'm going to take it up straight away or have a year's break to explore the world a bit. I need to juggle my finances a bit."

"You deserve a bit of a holiday after all that studying. Mind you, I remember you telling me about the night life as well, so it wasn't all hard work."

I laugh. "Well, I was at university. I needed to live a little."

"How's Victoria? I heard she's married now, and a Duchess as well."

"She is married. Nicholas is wonderful, and they're so happy. It's not public knowledge, yet, but they have a baby on the way."

"Oh, that's fantastic. You'll have to tell her to come by and see us soon. We've missed her. I can't believe her father never let her come here after he found out about the two male nurses we have. They're both happily married and were unlikely to be a threat to her innocence. Mind you, if his over protectiveness landed her a Duke, then who are we to complain?"

"Yes." It's the only word I can form. I can't tell her the full story of what a bastard Victoria's father is, and how she was lucky it was Nicholas she met and not someone like the old Duke. "I almost forgot..." I bluster, trying to disguise the quick change in direction of my conversation. "This is Nicholas' brother, William Cavendish, Earl Lullington. I've brought him to see the children."

"Oh my god. Why didn't you say sooner? I've only just got here. I didn't know we were having guests." Eve presents a little curtsy in front of William. "Your Earlship, it's wonderful to meet you. I'm Eve Kitchener. It's fabulous to have you come visit our little place."

"Please call me William." He extends his hand and accepting it, she shakes it. I know this is hard for him to do, making pleasant conversation when he'd rather be hidden away. "Tamara has told me she's been helping here since she was sixteen. I'm intrigued to meet the children."

"I'm sure you'll love them. They have their quirks, but they're all fantastic little human beings."

"I'm sure I will," William replies, and I can't help but smile toward him. He may think he's destined for the shadows, but he's being the perfect gentleman, and I haven't seen him tic once.

"Tamara"–Eve turns back to me– "I'll get you both badges, but have you warned William about some of the children and their possible reactions to things?"

The moment of truth. I swallow deeply and turn to William.

"You were asking me if this was a regular nursery. It isn't – it's a place for parents to bring their autistic children for interaction, advice, and help."

"Autistic?" The word leaves William's mouth the same time as his hand goes to his ear and flicks it.

"Yes."

"I see why you wanted to bring me and not Nicholas, then," he states bluntly, and I instantly see the regret cross his face at allowing the comment to escape.

"It isn't like that. I promise you."

Eve bites her lip and steps back to allow us some privacy.

"I don't need to see others like me to know I'm wired wrong."

"That's not why I brought you here. This place has been helping children ever since the onset of better diagnosis and understanding of autism, in the early nineties. You and I both know of the intolerance to it in your world. I just wanted you to see that in the wider world it's more common than you think. If you speak to any of the doctors here, they will tell you that with advances in assessment, it will be more common to be on the spectrum than not in a few years.

"But you know what I'm like?" William lowers his voice and leans into me.

"You won't hurt anyone here. Please. Just five minutes. If it's too much, we'll leave."

"Five minutes," William states as Eve comes back to us with badges, and I exhale the breath I've been holding since he realized the nature of the center we're now in.

"Please go through, they're expecting you." Eve smiles at me, and I nod a little thanks to her. William takes hold of my arm as I lead him through the security doors.

"I'm sorry I didn't tell you sooner."

"I need to know things, Tamara. I was prepared to meet normal children. I can already feel my heart beating faster because a surprise has been sprung on me. I can't handle them. You have to be honest with me, or you risk a meltdown."

"I didn't think you'd come if I told you the real reason."

"I probably wouldn't have," William responds truthfully. "But you have to give me a chance, and a choice."

"I will, next time."

William goes silent as we stand in front of another door. It's closed, but behind it, I can hear the happy chatter and laughter of children. He flicks his ear and then his nose. I give him a minute to compose himself, but his movements are getting worse. His fists clench then unclench in between the tics. I know he's struggling. I open my mouth and softly sing.

"Hush, little baby, don't say a word,
Mama's going to buy you a mocking bird.
And if that mockingbird don't sing,
Mama's going to buy you a diamond ring."

His fists unclench, and his arms lower to his side. He takes a deep inhalation and then nods.

"I'm ready."

I push open the door, and we are greeted with lots of happy, smiling faces. Many are children, but some are adults. The staff wear black t-shirts with a little puzzle piece in the corner. Off to the left is a room, which I know to be the sensory room. It's furnished with small beds, and there are soft bricks of varying sizes in it. The lights are low intensity and multi-colored. It's been purposefully designed, so it won't overstimulate the younger children, but it will allow them to play and explore. At the back of the main area is a computer room for the older children, containing a PlayStation and X-Box, along with several high spec Mac computers. They are monitored by staff because we once had a child who was so high functioning he tried to hack into MI5. I've watched some of the children in there before, and I'm amazed by the skills they possess in relation to coding and computer programing. I'm not in the least surprised everything is monitored by our tech genius, Dave. Off to the right is a small kitchen with a few tables for people to sit at and eat if they want to. Cooked meals can't be prepared here, but people can make sandwiches and the like. This area of the building is specifically for the day care parents. It's a place for mums and dads to come and talk to other parents as well as to highly trained staff members who are available at all times, offering advice. This is not all the center provides, though. It also has respite and permanent housing facilities for those who need a break or can't live alone. In fact, this place has everything needed to help those with autism live life to the fullest.

"Hello." A little boy stands at William's legs. I've seen him before and know him as Cory. He reaches out and touches the material of William's formal trousers before quickly pulling his hand back. His little face creases up as though he's musing on something, and then he reaches out and touches the fabric again. "I like your trousers."

Shifting my gaze to William I see his hand start to lift toward his face, but he stops its progression and instead holds it out to Cory.

"Hello, I'm William," he informs the little boy and kneels down, so he's at his level. "Can I tell you a secret? I like your trousers better." Cory looks down at his jogging bottoms and then back at William. "I usually like to be comfortable, but I thought I should dress up today. If I'd known you'd be wearing jogging bottoms, I would've as well."

A woman pushes through the crowd of people starting to assemble around us. She's Cory's mum.

"I'm so sorry," she apologizes, grabbing the little boy and pulling him to her. "He's got a thing about different fabrics. I hope he hasn't made your trousers dirty."

"Please. It doesn't matter. I was just telling him I wish I'd worn my jogging bottoms like him. I feel overdressed."

"You're an important man. I'm sure nobody minds what you wear." The young mum blushes, and I try to stifle a laugh when I realize she thinks William is attractive. Certainly, with his broad shoulders, imposing height, and stunning good looks, he's the most desirable man I've ever met.

"Thank you." William immediately looks down to the ground, not being sure how to handle the compliment.

"Cory." A little girl approaches us. I scan my brain, struggling to recall her name, but when she places her hands on her hips, I see the supports on her wrists and remember straight away this is Lexie. As well as being on the spectrum, she also has hyper-mobility and dyspraxia. "You weren't supposed to touch the Earl. That's what they told us during the talk this morning. They said smile politely, don't touch him, and don't talk to him unless he speaks to you first. We have to follow the rules."

"I didn't mean to." Cory's little bottom lip quivers as though he's going to cry. "I couldn't help it. I needed to know what his trousers felt like."

Lexie keeps her hands on her hips, and for a minute I think she's going to tell the poor boy off again. She doesn't though, instead, she gives him a cuddle, and then pulls him off to play with his still blushing mother in tow.

"You ok?" I check with William.

"Yes. You know I did the same thing once. My father had a guest he was trying to con out of money, and the man had on these velvet looking trousers. I really wanted to know what they felt like. The only problem was I'd been painting with my nanny. When they entered the nursery, my hands were covered in bright green paint, and I smeared it all over his trousers when I touched him. My father didn't get the money he wanted, and I got a hiding and relegated to my room for a few days. We were never allowed paints in the house again." He looks down at his hands as though remembering the green paint that was once on them. "Maybe, I should ask Nicholas if we can get some?"

"Why ask? If you want something just get it."

William turns his head to look at me as though he can't quite understand what I'm saying.

"It's Nicholas' house. I have to obey his rules."

"Has he told you that?" I question.

"No, but it's just what happens."

I fall silent and make a mental note to tell Nicholas of this revelation when I return to the house. I'm pretty certain he'd prefer William to have whatever he wanted and not have to ask for it.

"Tamara…Earl Lullington." One of the doctor's steps forward and presents a little bow to William who shakes his hand. "My name is Dr. Brown. It's lovely to have you both here. The children have been very excited since Tamara's call earlier. Tamara is very popular with them, and I'm sure you will be loved as well, My Lord."

"Please. Call me William. 'My Lord' is for my slightly more formal and stubborn brother."

"Of course. Has Tamara told you details of our facilities?"

William looks toward me.

"I've given him a brief tour and overview," I offer by way of an explanation.

"Not a problem. Our facilities here are for children and adults with formal diagnosis on the spectrum. We don't turn anyone away, though. We simply help them liaise with the appropriate doctors to find a solution. We currently have ten long-term residents, varying in age and range of diagnosis." The doctor starts to walk through the rooms, showing everything to William as he goes. I stand back and observe him as he takes it all in. He asks many sensible questions, and I can see he's finally relaxing after the initial shock.

"I'm not sure if Tamara has told you, but I'm on the spectrum myself." William tells the doctor.

"She hasn't, but I've seen in your mannerisms and lack of eye contact that you might be. I've worked most of my life with children and adults, having all levels of diagnosis, so I recognize the traits straight away."

"I'm that obvious." William laughs nervously.

"Not at all. For someone with different social behaviors to the norm, you are doing extremely well."

"Thank you," William offers, and I gently take his hand. He allows me to do so and wraps his fingers around mine.

"Can I ask you something?" William says as he steps aside to let a little child go running past with headphones on to shield against the noise.

"Of course, please, if I can help in anyway?"

"How much does having autism shape who you are? Can it cause a darkness within you?"

The doctor opens and shuts his eyes rapidly, shocked at the question.

"That's a difficult question. There have been people who've committed crimes and have either had issues before or are subsequently diagnosed to be on the spectrum, but autism doesn't make someone inherently evil. It's just a question of different wiring. In relation to the nature versus nurture debate, I believe any darkness comes from the way someone is raised and their life experiences rather than innately from birth. I don't think you have to worry about an evil side though. I've found over the years that Tamara is an excellent judge of character, and so are some of these children. They've warmed to you already, which demonstrates to me the make-up of the person you are." The doctor smiles at William and I know inside his head his thoughts must be going a mile a minute. The doctor lowers his head in a bow again before returning to a nearby mum, trying to calm a distressed child whose jigsaw piece is missing.

"Do you want to go?" I look up at William. We are still holding hands.

He shakes his head.

"No. I like it here. It's calming."

"They do wonders. I'm so glad I found it."

William gazes out across the people in the room, and I see

his stare focus in on a father and son. They are cuddling up together on a chair, reading a book about space together. His face goes blank, and I can no longer read his emotions.

"It was him all along. It was never me." He bends down and presses a kiss to my head. "I wasn't the one who was wrong."

CHAPTER FIFTEEN

WILLIAM

*S*itting at the breakfast table shoveling my Weetabix into my mouth, I keep staring down at the small piece of paper in front of me. It's a picture drawn by Cory from the center the other day. It's of me and him lying on the floor in the sensory room staring at the lights. We must've lain there together for at least half an hour just saying the color of the lights or a variation when they changed. He was really impressed with my knowledge of the color wheel and even more that I knew of a blue-green color called zomp. He'd always wanted to know if you could get a color for every letter of the alphabet. I was hesitant at first when I found out the center was for those on the autism spectrum, but the more time I've spent there, the more confident I've become. Although at the same time a sadness has developed within me when I see the interactions and the love between the children and their parents, reminding me of what I didn't have growing up. To be different is not the scandal or embarrassment my father led me to believe. It's something to be cherished, making the person unique. I need to try and keep that thought in my head.

My brother pops his head over my shoulder. "Good picture, little brother, but I'm not sure you are up to the standard of Van Gogh, just yet. I'm uncertain whether Victoria's critical eye will accept it as a replacement for the 'Poppies'." He laughs at his unfunny joke.

"It's not mine. It was drawn by one of the children at the day care center," I reply testily.

"I know." Nicholas chuckles. "If it was your drawing, it would be so much worse."

I snort my frustration and folding the picture up, I tuck it in my pocket. I think I'll get a frame for it and put it up on the wall in my room, later.

"Has Victoria got her head down the toilet again this morning?" I ask my brother with blunt honesty.

"You've such a delicate way with words, but you always speak the truth. I left her trying to eat a ginger biscuit to settle her poor stomach. I think I'll get a doctor out to her today. This has been going on far too long now," he says, shaking his head. The butler steps forward and pulls out a seat for my brother to take his position at the head of the table for breakfast. "I'll have two slices of toast with a piece of bacon, two poached eggs, and a large coffee please. The Duchess will also be down in a minute. She'll have a slice of toast and lemon water please." My brother turns to me, "What do you think Tamara will want?"

I shrug and push my finished bowl of cereal away.

"Food?"

"Helpful." He rolls his eyes. "Bring Miss Bennett the same as me, but with one egg."

"At once, Your Grace." The butler scurries away.

"I miss Reggie," Nicholas states flatly. "He would have known immediately what Tamara wanted."

"I know."

We both fall silent in memory of our previous butler and stand-in father figure who was killed during Victoria's trials.

"I don't give a fuck if he's taking his breakfast. I'll see him now, or I'll shove your head through this god damn door." I instantly recognize the not so dulcet tones of Lord West, coming from out in the hallway.

"He must have received the legal letters from Tamara." My brother pushes back his chair and prepares to greet our uninvited breakfast guest. I remain seated, continuing to eat my toast.

The dining room door bursts open and ricochets off the wall behind it. An antique vase on a nearby table wobbles but doesn't fall.

"I will ruin you, Oakfield." Lord West storms into the room. He's dressed in a navy blue, formal suit and brandishes an umbrella in his hand.

"I believe it is you who'll be ruined, West," my brother replies with a bored nonchalance. "In accordance with the letter, unless you comply with the new rules of the society, you will be ejected and will forfeit assets to pay the subsequent fines as a result."

"I'll do nothing of the fucking sort. Just because you're too much of a wimp to run the society as it should be and has always been, it doesn't mean we'll allow you to ruin all our hard work and fun."

"Fun!" my brother spits out. "Have you met my wife and seen all the trials she had to go through."

Lord West smirks. "Yes, I've met her, and I seem to remember how good her perky little tits felt in my hands. Shame I never got a chance to savor her pussy."

Nicholas steps forward, prepared to make Lord West pay for his statement, but I'm on my feet quickly and place myself between the two.

"No," I tell my brother. "He's baiting you."

"Yeah, Nicholas. Listen to your freak of a brother. Hit me and I'll have you arrested for assault. Another reason for me to gather a 'no confidence' vote in you as the leader." West waits a heartbeat before continuing to antagonize my brother. "I'm sure Viscount Hamilton would make a perfect new leader. After all he'll be able to keep his bitch of a daughter in control better than you can."

My brother struggles harder in my arms, and I'm on the verge of not being able to control him when I hear Tamara's authoritative voice. Seeing her so near to this man, and knowing what he's capable of, sends shivers down my spine.

"Lord West." Tamara steps into the room with her head held high while Victoria lingers in the doorway behind her, looking white as a sheet. Tamara's dressed in a tight skirt and blouse with a jacket over it. Her long black hair is pulled back in a bun at the nape of her neck, and she looks every inch the professional lawyer... fuck...she's hot as hell. "I must advise you that I've just recorded every word of slander you've made against my client, the Duchess of Oakfield." She holds up her phone, and I can't help but smirk at her genius. "In it, you've also admitted to touching the Duchess inappropriately. I'm sure if she were to give me a statement to that effect, then a court of law might find you guilty of sexual assault. Furthermore, should His Grace, the Duke of Oakfield, escape his brother's restricting arms and feel the need to administer a punch to your face – one, which given his strength and current demeanor, would be likely to damage your good looks via a broken nose, then I'm sure a court of law would also find he had due cause to protect his wife's good character and person. Especially having heard your previous admission of sexual assault upon her person." Tamara moves closer to Lord West as I let go of Nicholas who's stopped struggling in my arms. I step back into the shadows and can feel myself getting hard at Tamara's majestic display. I've thought her a weak woman before, but here in this room, she's commanding and authoritative. It's the biggest turn on ever. She could match me blow for blow in a duel of words. Maybe she is the woman for me and could handle the darkness within me.

"I suggest you leave this place immediately. At the very least, the recording I've made will be enough to have a restraining order put in place against you. I'm certain that would affect your ability to continue as an active member of the Oakfield Society despite its unlawful conception and activities." Standing directly in front of Lord West, Tamara places both of her hands on her hips and stares him down.

"Damn." West grabs his groin and re-arranges it in front of us all. "That made me so fucking hard. Do you talk like that in the bedroom?"

"I'm still recording, Lord West," Tamara counters while my

fists clench ready to attack should West make any attempt to hurt the woman in front of him. My protective instincts are flooding through my body, but they are also joined by feelings of darkness, which shroud me in their shadows. Lord West finds her display a turn on, and so do I. He is evil incarnate, but I'm experiencing the same responses as him. Surely, this proves how dark and dangerous my soul is.

"You, my darling, will be fun to break," he sneers and turns his attention to Nicholas. "Oakfield, remove the sanctions against me and desist with your plans, or you'll regret it. I won't rest until I take everything from you. This house, your wife, your hot little lawyer, and even your brother. How would you like it if I get him locked up under the Mental Health Act for some of his past perverted deeds?" West's laugh sucks all the air out of the room, and I know he's referring to the incident with the girl in my bedroom. My heart is starting to beat rapidly, the air in my lungs feels cold and seems to lack oxygen. My head clouds with a foggy haze of emotions: anger, protectiveness, fear. The stimulation is too much. I know I'm rocking, and I know I'm tic'ing. "Are you videoing this one, Miss Bennett? There's all the proof needed to demonstrate that William Cavendish is not safe to be allowed free in society."

I can hear the words being spoken around me. More angry exchanges then doors slamming before silence. West has gone. His evil presence is no longer constricting the aura of the room. Now there's only mine, flowing and twisting around the edges of the royally decorated room like black plumes of smoke. It's as if the dementors from Harry Potter are pulling me under their spell.

"Victoria, get me a sedative, quickly," Nicholas calls out, and it permeates my bewildered brain.

"Wait." I hear Tamara say, and I can feel her getting closer to me.

"No!" I shout, bringing my hands up in front of my face. "That was beautiful. You were so majestic. But, I'm like him." I bring my hand down to my groin and can feel the hardness there.

"It's not wrong, William. I promise you. It excites me to know you liked my display." Tamara is speaking, and I know she's near, but she sounds so far away.

"Hush, little baby, don't say a word,
Mama's going to buy you a mocking bird.
And if that mockingbird don't sing,
Mama's going to buy you a diamond ring."

I feel a finger touch the top of my nose. It's soft and tender, and while Tamara continues to sing, it is stroked down to the tip and then back up.

"I'm here, William. Nothing's wrong…I promise you. Nicholas and Victoria are here as well. West has gone. You're *not* him."

I stop rocking and allow her words to sink in. *"I'm not him. I'm NOT him."* I shut my eyes and take a deep breath before opening them again. My mind has cleared, and my meltdown has been averted without the need for a sedative. I've responded to Tamara. She's talked me down when I needed her to. Reaching out, she takes my hand.

"How do you feel?" she asks, and I blink a few times to center myself further.

"Good. Thank you."

"You're not a bad man, William. Just because you liked my little display of power doesn't make you anything like West."

Nicholas steps forward.

"Hell, little brother. I liked her display too. I might have to take Victoria upstairs and get her to talk all legal-like to me." Nicholas chuckles.

"That's probably a case of too much information." Tamara screws her face up.

"I'm sorry," I tell them both. "Everything is different from what I'm used to. The world is a crazy place and so vibrant. Sometimes, I can't fully handle everything around me."

Tamara leans into me, and I wrap my arms around her shoulders.

"That's what you have us for. Everyone has their mad moments. It's what you do after that counts."

She looks up at me, her eyes wide with both wonder and the affection she holds for me. For the first time ever, I don't see any fear. It's gone because I'm finally accepting my needs. It's then I realize that everything Tamara has been doing has been for a reason. She's been helping me to discover the life I can have outside the confines of my father's rules, giving me the chance to be myself, not a monster created by him. Leaning forward, I press a kiss to the top of her forehead just as Victoria comes running into the room with a hypodermic filled with sedative.

"Damn!" she exclaims. "I hate being pregnant. I spend all day throwing up and then get to miss all the good things."

We all laugh, and Nicholas strides confidently over to her.

"How about I take you upstairs and show you something good."

"If it's your dick, then I think I'll pass. It's got a lot to answer for at the moment!"

Tamara rests her head against my chest as we watch the

comic interaction between husband and wife. With him trying to get laid, and his pregnant wife informing him she's never opening her legs for him again. For the first time in forever, I feel calm… natural…normal.

CHAPTER SIXTEEN

TAMARA

"Do you want another romantic comedy, or can we have something with a bit more action in it?" William flicks between the Netflix icon of *Fast and Furious* and *Crazy, Stupid Love*.

"You can put the car one on." I shake my head at him. "I'm done with romance for the day. Although I will have to tell you all the laws they're breaking in the film."

"Deal." William switches back to *Fast and Furious* and sets it up to play. He pauses the screen, though. "Do you want anything more to eat or drink?"

We've been watching films for the last few hours. Ever since the clash with Lord West this morning, nobody has felt like doing much. Nicholas arranged for a doctor to come and see Victoria about her morning sickness. She was prescribed some pills and, along with Nicholas, took to her rooms for some rest. I suspect she was also breaking her vow to never allow her husband near her again, especially when chocolate coated strawberries were sent to their room. I can't take my friend anywhere. Mind you, it's lovely to see her so happy. William and I took a walk around the estate to clear his head after his almost meltdown this morning. We sent the driver to fetch a traditional takeaway kebab for lunch because I'd discovered during the walk William had never had one before. The Oakfield's chef wasn't impressed, and I'm not sure William was either. I kept reassuring him it tasted better after a night out drinking at the pub. I don't think he believed me. The chef made us a platter of snacks, and we came into the cinema room to watch films for the afternoon. Following his kiss to my forehead this morning, we've not engaged in any other embraces but simply enjoyed being close to each other. It had been a perfect afternoon, and I didn't want it to end.

"Do you think the chef has any more of those chocolate cookies?" I rub my index finger through the crumbs on the plate and lick them off my digit.

William presses a button located in the arm of the comfortable sofa we're sitting on, and the voice of the chef fills the room.

"My Lord?"

"Do you happen to have any more chocolate cookies left?" William asks.

"I've just taken a fresh batch out of the oven." I can tell the chef is happy to be cooking, and I can imagine him sniffing the freshly baked smell into his nostrils.

"Can you send some for Miss Bennett, please?"

"Of course. Anything for you, sir?"

"I'll just have another coffee, thank you. Best make it decaffeinated, though, or I'll be awake all night."

"I'll bring them right through."

"Has Nicholas said whether he'll be taking dinner downstairs or in his rooms, yet?" William asks.

"I believe he's eating downstairs, but I've not been able to confirm that. He was called into an urgent meeting, according to the butler."

"Urgent meeting?" I see William's brows furrow together. I love the concern he has for his brother. The two of them are beyond close. I often wonder if it's what got them through their youth, making them the men they are today. The bond between them being strengthened with everything that was thrown at them.

"Yes, sir. I believe it was..." The chef goes quiet.

"Was who?"

"I can't say." The jovial nature of the chef has completely disappeared, and his voice is caged.

"Now," William orders, his voice terse and commanding. "I want details. Now!"

"I believe it was Miss Bennett's mother."

William turns his head to look at me, and my mouth must fall open in shock. Before I know it, I'm gasping like a fish out of water, trying to find words. William grabs my hand, and we are running through the corridors of Oakfield Hall toward the office we all share. Without knocking, William barges in. My mother is sitting in a chair with Victoria. My friend's arm is around her, and my mother's crying.

"Mum," I call, and I'm across the room in an instant and at

her feet checking her for injuries. "What's wrong? What's happened?"

I look up at Nicholas and see the frown on his face. He looks over toward William and shakes his head.

"Tamara, why don't we wait outside? This could be nothing, but I'm sure Nicholas can handle it." William taps me on the shoulder and tries to assist me to my feet, but I jerk away from him.

"My mother is crying. I'm not going anywhere until someone tells me what's going on."

"She...came to apologize to me...for knowing about my father's plans and not helping me," Victoria stutters her answer quickly, too quickly, and I see it instantly for the lie it is. She's pale, shaking, and has also been crying.

"You told me she wouldn't know I've been here." My mother looks up at Nicholas while using a tissue in her hand to dab away the tears in her eyes.

"I'm sorry, Ms. Bennett. When William goes in the cinema room, he's usually in there for hours watching films. I truly didn't know they'd find out you were here."

"Will you stop talking like I'm not here and tell me what is going on? I have a right to know."

My mum lets out a long sob, and I squeeze her hand tightly.

"Whatever it is, Mummy, I can help you. Is it the Viscount? Has he done something to you after our last visit? If he's fired you, you're better off away from that place. Victoria wants you here. I want you here."

She shakes her head and inhales a whimper, trying to dampen it down, so it doesn't explode into a full-blown cry of anguish.

"I never wanted you to find out. I thought if Nicholas knew, he could protect you. It's the only reason I took the risk."

"Find out what? Mum, you're not making any sense?"

Victoria gets to her feet and going over to her husband, buries her head in his chest. I can hear her sobbing.

"Please, my darling daughter, you have to forgive me."

"Forgive you? If you mean, knowing about Victoria, then of course. I was mad at you the other day, but I know without your protection Victoria would have suffered even worse from her father. It turned out alright for her and Nicholas anyway. Mum, you're forgiven. Of course, you are." I get up and bring her into my arms, but she cries harder, and I can hear her whimpering, 'no'.

"Tamara. You need to let your mother speak," Nicholas orders, and I pull back from her in confusion before sitting next to her on the sofa. I search her face for answers, trying to read the lines of age on her weathered features. She looks so tired and old. To me, she's always been young, but in this moment, I see her for a woman who's had to deal with a lot in her life. I know instinctively what she has to tell me. William must as well for I feel his comforting warmth getting closer to me.

"My father?" I question not really wanting answers.

"Yes." Her voice is almost a whisper, but to me, it's as loud as a fog horn, sounding out a warning for ships to avoid the rocks that will shatter them and send them into the depths of tempestuous seas.

"You know who he is?"

She nods.

"I'll always remember the night you were conceived. I see it vividly in my dreams, every night. It's haunted me all these years. The day had started out perfectly. Having completed my work, I'd been given half a day off, and I went to the cinema. I'd always been a James Bond fan and was desperate to see the new one, *Golden Eye*. I loved it. He might be a little bit older than me, but Pierce Brosnan is a handsome man. I wandered back home in a bit of a daydream. I was working for the Viscount by then. Master Theodore had just been born and the Viscountess was resting after the birth. I went into the kitchen to get a drink. The Viscount was there."

My stomach sinks. In my heart, I know where this story is heading, but I don't want it to go there. Damn, I don't want it to be true. Please god, let me wake up and find this was a nightmare.

"We spoke for a while. Just general conversation. He asked me about the film, and I couldn't hide my crush on James Bond. The Viscount laughed at me and told me James Bond wasn't a real man because that wasn't how to treat a woman. He told me that if a real man took a woman as a lover, he'd make sure that they knew he'd been there. Breaking them forever. I joked that I thought Bond was renowned for that, and then he lurched forward and grabbed me, pinning me to the kitchen counter. I'll remember his words until the day I die.

'Not that sort of broken, but actually physically and mentally rip that pussy up, so no man can stick his dick in it again. Breaking her until she knows that all she is is a hole for a man to use and own.'

I'm vaguely aware of William sitting down behind me and placing his hands on my shoulders. I need his strength because I'm drowning in the revelations.

"The Viscount placed his hand under the denim skirt I was wearing and moved it up toward my private parts. I protested and tried to stop him, but his strength was too much for me.

He pinned me down, ripped my underwear off, and did exactly what he said he would do. He broke me physically and mentally."

"And got you pregnant with me?" Tears start to stream down my cheeks. My heart is broken, and my head aches.

My mother nods.

"It's why when you and Victoria used to joke you were sisters from another mother, I would disappear to my room and cry for hours. You are sisters, half anyway, sharing the same father."

"Viscount Hamilton is my father?...He raped you?" I can barely get the words out. I'm still trying to will myself to wake up from this nightmare. It can't be true. It can't be. "William." I reach around, and as he pulls me to him, I start to cry. I cry for the years I fantasized about who my father could be. Maybe a soldier who died in battle, and my mother couldn't bear to tell me because she was so heartbroken at his loss, or a traveler with whom my mother had a brief fairytale romance. After he'd left, she'd discovered my existence and although she'd no way to contact him, it didn't matter because she had a part of him with her forever. No, the reality is horrible, disgusting, and sick. I'm the result of a brutal attack on my mother by a man so vile he needs to be sent to hell. He's ruined my mother's life, given his own daughter away, and he's bought a woman who's disappeared without trace. Even his own wife was purchased for him. I can only imagine what other atrocities he's committed in his life. I push away from William and get to my feet. I need air...I can't breathe. I open a window, and sticking my head out of it, I gulp the sweet oxygen into my lungs, but they don't seem to fill quickly enough. William comes up behind me and turning me to face him, he strokes his finger down the tip of his my nose.

"*Hush, little baby...*" He doesn't need to say the rest, I instantly succumb to his solace.

"How can I be his daughter?"

William wipes away my tears.

"I can't..." I start, but he hushes me with his finger against my lips.

"You can. You have to. I'm with you all the way."

I look around his colossal frame to where my mother sits, looking tiny on the sofa. Victoria is still crying into Nicholas' arms. She's my sister, something I've wanted all my life, and that wish just came true, but not in the way I'd hoped.

I nod at William, indicating I'm doing alright. I've collected myself and need to continue my conversation with my mother. He leads me back to the chair, and I take my mother's hands within mine when I sit. William sits behind me.

"I'm sorry, Tammy. I never wanted you to know this. I wanted to take it to my grave, so it wouldn't hurt you. I wanted you to think you had a father who loved me, and you were conceived out of love."

"You can't always protect me from the monsters, Mum. I need the truth. I'm going to go up against this man and destroy him for what he's done to Victoria and you." My calm outer voice disguises the quivering fear inside me at undertaking such a feat. "Why did you stay with him? Why not leave?"

"Where could I go? I had nobody else. Your grandparents weren't always around. My job was my life, and my color still a hindrance. The Viscount offered me a future despite what he'd done. A future, which included him paying for your education. I couldn't turn that down. It's one of the reasons I always made you study so hard because I wanted it to cost him as much as possible. To make him suffer financially even just in a small way. I was so proud of you for getting into Cambridge. I knew that one day you'd be able to put an end to the society and their old fashioned, evil ways. Use this news to spur you on, Tamara. Don't let it destroy the strength I know you have inside you."

"I won't, Mum. You have my word on that. We will both stand triumphant over the Viscount one day."

My mother and I embrace, again, but this time stay together and cry. The others in the room stand in silence, allowing us this moment to begin the healing process. Eventually, my mother pulls back.

"I've given Nicholas evidence from that night." Her eyes flick to a package rolled up on her desk. I realize it must be the clothes she was wearing. "I kept everything in case I needed it. There's a sworn statement and a couple of photos. It will remain as my word against his, and I know staying in his employment will count against me, but if it helps in anyway, it's there to use."

"We will keep it safe and use it against him." Nicholas says, tapping his hand on the desk next to the evidence. I immediately feel sick, knowing what will be contained within the package. I think I'll allow the men to deal with that as much as possible.

"What happens now? Nicholas, we need to get my mother somewhere safe?"

I can instantly tell from the Duke's expression that hiding her away is not part of his plan.

"No," I tell him in no uncertain terms. "There's no way I'm allowing her to go back to that house."

"It's not my decision, Tamara," Nicholas tells me, and I whip my head around to my mother.

"I have to. I believe the Viscount is planning something for Theodore, and I can't allow him to hurt that boy after what he did to Victoria. Theo doesn't know anything about the society. Viscount Hamilton has weaved a web of lies and deceit to trap the boy. I think whatever is happening may involve the missing girl from the sale, as well – the one the Viscount purchased. I've not seen her, but I know he has her. I have to try and find out what's happening."

"But it's too risky. What if he finds out you've been here? He was already suspicious when we visited the other day."

"Which was why I went along with his plans that day to upset you, making you think I'm a bad person. It was the only way."

"Mum, this is too dangerous," I plead.

"Nicholas is going to put protection in place for me. It may take a few days, but hopefully I'll be able to get the information I need by then and get out."

"I don't like it," I tell her like a petulant child, and she lets out a soft chuckle.

"I know." She strokes her hand over my head. "I don't either, but I don't have a choice. He may have broken me that night, but he also gave me a special gift. One that'll help protect me until my dying breath."

"Don't." I shake my head, not wanting to hear talk of her death.

Mum squeezes my hands one final time and gets up onto her feet.

"I'm so proud of you, of the woman you've become." She looks behind me to William and then back to me. "And the woman you'll become. You're in safe hands here at Oakfield Hall." Victoria comes over and embraces her. "You both are. I know you'll always be happy. That's all I've ever wanted."

CHAPTER SEVENTEEN

WILLIAM

I sit at my desk in the study, watching as Tamara flicks around the screen on her desk. It's been twenty-hours since her mother left, and she's barely spoken to anyone. I don't even think she slept last night because she's in the same clothes as yesterday. Before we'd watched the film, she'd changed from her business suit into jeans and a jumper, and she's still wearing them. Victoria and Nicholas huddle together over the other side of the room, reading through a document Nicholas drafted for the new constitution of the society.

I slide out of my plush leather chair, having done little

more than play Roblox on my computer for the last hour, and pour a glass of water from the jug, which is resting on top of a seventeenth century sideboard. I take the glass over to Tamara and place it in front of her.

"You've not drunk anything for a while. It's bad for you. You'll get dehydrated, and then you'll get a headache. If it gets really bad, you could end up in hospital on a drip. I know because I've read all about it." I want to slap myself in the face for having verbal diarrhea, but the smile crossing her face makes me feel less stupid. "Sorry."

"Don't be. I do need to drink." She looks back at her computer screen, then turns it to face me. I see it's on the ancestry page she was looking at the other day, and I notice her name and Theodore's on the screen. It says the probability of them being half brother and sister is high. "I guess we don't need to do an official DNA test. This proves it."

"I guess." I shrug, wanting to comfort her, but the words fail me. My social sensibilities are virtually non-existent at times like this. It's a curse but also a blessing. "Does that make you my half sister-in-law?"

"Possibly. I don't know how it works. I'll have to Google it." Tamara pulls up a fresh browser and starts to type while I hum a thought. "What is it?"

"Well. It doesn't make it illegal for me to fuck you does it?"

She can't help the laugh that escapes her lips. It's loud, refreshing, and much needed. Causing Victoria and Nicholas to look up from the document they are engrossed in.

"Thank you." She laughs again.

"What for?"

"Being you."

"I'm not always certain that's a good thing but alright."

"It's exactly what I needed."

"What's going on?" Victoria inquires with enthusiasm.

"William's being perfect," Tamara responds, getting to her feet and embracing me.

"Should I even ask what he said?" Nicholas wraps his arms around his wife.

"The right thing. He said the right thing."

"Cryptic. Definitely a lawyer." Nicholas rolls his eyes.

"Well can I?" I bring the conversation back to my question. I want to know the answer. It's important.

"Yes, William. If I say you can fuck me, you can. It's not illegal because we don't share any common blood."

"Hey, who are you saying has common blood? I've got the blood of Dukes, remember," Nicholas retorts with a chuckle. I like the fact the tension of the last twenty-four hours is starting to dissipate.

"I guess my blood's not as common as I thought it was either." Tamara sticks her tongue out at Victoria and my brother, her half brother-in-law. This is going to get so confusing and give me a headache. I'm going to have to develop a family tree to figure out how all the links work. It will bug me if not, and that only leads to trouble, or several hours spent distracting myself by trying to name as many facts as I can about space or the United States of America. My record is six hours discussing Florida with myself when I was trying to forget how Prince John was related to Marie Antoinette. Damn it. I'm going to get that thought in my head, again. I knew he was her fifth cousin seven times removed or something, and I drew a big diagram to prove it. Nicholas became frustrated because it took up too much space in the playroom, and in the end, he burned it.

Victoria bites her lip. "How do you feel? I mean...about us sharing blood? What my...our father did?"

"I can't lie and say I don't want to kill him with my bare hands for what he did to my mother. But, to be honest, I'm not surprised it was him. It makes sense being the type of man he is. He gave you up for financial gain to a society, which would've raped and killed you if it weren't for Nicholas being the man destined to inherit the title. I'm worried sick about my mother still being in the house, and everything that could happen to her, but I understand why she's gone back. Theodore is just as much an innocent in all of this as you and my mother were. He's being manipulated by the Viscount, and we need to put a stop to it. I'll never call him father but to know you're my sister is the best news I've ever had. It cements what we've known all along."

"I feel the same. I'm sad but happy at the same time. It's confusing." A smile breaks out across her face.

"Oh." Tamara claps her hands excitedly. "I just thought of something."

"What?" I ask at the same time as Victoria.

"The baby inside you. I know I was going to be its cool Auntie Tamara who let it get away with everything Mummy and Daddy won't, but I 'll really be this baby's aunt."

"You will." Victoria pats her still flat tummy.

"Oh my god. I hope it's a girl. I can take her shopping, and we can spend all Nicholas' money."

Nicholas puts his head in his hands and groans.

"William, help me here."

"Better a girl than a boy. If it's a boy, Uncle William will spend all Daddy's money on Lego to build with him."

"I'm doomed." Nicholas throws his hands up in the air and goes back over to his desk to resume reading the society's documentation. Tamara and Victoria continue giggling between them. I can hear something about first dates if the baby is a girl with Nicholas standing guard like a mafia hitman looking after the Don's daughter. I'm actually hoping for a little girl. After generations dominated by men, it'll be refreshing to take the family name in a different direction. Mind you, Uncle William will be standing right next to Nicholas, protecting his niece.

Tamara stretches, then yawns. I can see the tension has finally been dispelled from her body, and exhaustion is taking over.

"Why don't you go and have a nap?" I half question and half demand.

"I think I will. I could do with a shower as well." She lifts her arm and sniffs. "I'm surprised one of you hasn't already dumped me in a bath, because I smell so bad."

"I didn't think you'd appreciate it. I don't see you as a wet t-shirt competition type of lady," I tease, and she bats out at me playfully.

Victoria coughs. "Sorry to interrupt..." –She winks at us– "Tammy, can I sleep with you? I'm really tired, and I know Nicholas wants to finish looking at this document. I'm just...you know..."

"Of course..." –Tamara wraps her arm around her friend – "Sister." She tests the word on her lips, and I know from the smile reaching the corners of her eyes she enjoys it.

"See you later, ladies." I bow at them, and they leave the room. I look over to Nicholas who's got a frown on his face as he studies the documentation in front of him.

"Something wrong?" I ask and drag my chair over to his table.

"No. I just want to make sure everything is correct, and there are no possible loopholes."

"I'll read through it later. You know how pedantic I can be at times."

"Don't I just."

He tips his head toward the door.

"Bit of a shock for them both. Do you think they'll be ok?"

"We're living with two of the strongest women I know. They've been through shit and still come out the other side laughing and taking the piss out of us. They'll be absolutely fine. We need to get Elsie out of the Viscount's house as soon as possible, though. It's dangerous for her there."

"I know. I hated letting her go back. I wanted to put my foot down, but I think Tamara's stubborn streak definitely comes from her mother, and not her father."

"Oh, yes."

Nicholas opens the drawer to his desk and pulls out a bottle of whiskey and two glasses. Pouring out a glass for each of us, he hands me one, and I hold it up in a toast to his health. He does the same to me.

"I've not had a chance to ask you how you're coping with everything? There's a lot going on at the moment, and with you now having the freedom to be your own man, I wondered if you were managing ok? I've seen Tamara calm you down a few times, now." Nicholas takes a sip of his drink and then holds it to his nose, so he can inhale the honeyed scent.

"It's strange. Some days are better than others."

"I can understand that."

"The day care center was an eye opener. I realized autism is a lot more common than I originally believed. Our father often made me feel as though I was the only person with it in the world."

"I'm glad she took you."

"So am I." I place my glass down on the table. "I've been

doing some research since I left. There are a number of places like that around the country. I spoke to the manager of one. He was really friendly." I pause, unsure of how to proceed with what I have to say. I don't need to worry though. My brother's always been able to read me like a book.

"You're leaving Oakfield, aren't you?" he asks – his face solemn.

"I think I need to. Maybe just for the short term. It could be longer, I don't know. These four walls carry so many bad memories for me, and I need to figure out who I can be when I'm not surrounded by them."

He nods.

"You've applied for a place?"

"I have. I've been accepted as well. I can go whenever I want."

Nicholas places his own drink down on his desk.

"Whatever you need. You know I'll always support you. Just make sure it's somewhere I can visit whenever I need to get away from a pregnant wife."

"Of course."

We both stand up at the same time.

"You're my little brother, William. I'm always here for you. I know you need to discover yourself, but you'll always have a home here."

"Thank you."

Nicholas and I have never been touchy feely people, it's not how we were brought up, but the embrace complete with backslapping, which now passes between us feels right.

CHAPTER EIGHTEEN

TAMARA

"For you." William puts a large wad of paper down in front of me.

"What's this?" I flip over the first few sheets and see they're bank statements. My eyes scan to the name at the top: Viscount Arthur Hamilton. "How on Earth did you get these? Actually, no, don't tell me. Everything about the code of ethics I operate under says I shouldn't even be looking at these."

"I'm sure if something has come from MI5, then it can't be deemed to be too illegal." William winks at me and sifts through the papers until he reaches a page on which he's stuck a Post-it-note. "I think it's probably a decoy, but the Viscount has been paying an amount once a week to this lady."

He produces another smaller wad of paper and puts it in front of me.

"Camilla Fentress. She's been interesting to research because she's not a real person."

"Not a real person?" I screw my nose up in confusion and scrutinize the information in front of me. Camilla's name is in bold at the top of the page. Underneath is a picture of a woman who can't be much older than twenty.

"Nope. It's a company. This is actually a photo of a woman named Lindsey Sharp, originally from Missouri. Three years ago, she traveled to Los Angeles to make her fortune, but I've discovered she never made it to LA. She disappeared and hasn't been seen or heard from since."

He flicks through the bank statements again and stops at another marked page. "This statement is from around the time when she disappeared."

I look down at the information in front of me and instantly see a cash withdrawal from an ATM in Missouri.

"The Viscount was there?"

"Yes. He was there and is now using a picture of her with a fake identity. If you ask me, something doesn't add up, and that's not just because I've got a mathematical brain."

"No. We need to research this Lindsay Sharp some more and see how she became a company called Camilla Fentress." I flick over the pages of the report William's given me on Camilla. There's nothing concrete in there to go on, yet.

"That's why I'm not just a pretty face. I've already got our contacts on it. This could be a lead on the missing girl Joanna, or it could be nothing. But I'm going to pursue it."

I reach out and take his hand.

"I think you're actually enjoying playing detective."

He shrugs.

"Maybe, a little."

A stray hair tumbles out of the small bun at the nape of my neck. William reaches around and tucks it back in. His hand lingers at my chin, and I feel the heat of his body warm mine with desire. He leans into me and our lips meet in a quick kiss.

He pulls back. Neither of us speak – we just sit in silence, staring at each other. Sticking my tongue slightly out of my mouth, I lick what was left behind of his taste. He leans in again, but we're stopped by an abrupt knock at the door. William stands up and rearranges his trousers.

"Come in," he says as he looks wistfully over his shoulder at me.

The door opens, and the butler enters.

"My apologies, sir. The Duke and Duchess are still at their charity lunch, and there's a man here demanding to speak to either the Duke or you."

"Who is it?" William asks, and I turn back to the documentation in front of me, allowing him privacy to talk with the butler.

"It's the police, sir."

"Police?"

"Yes, sir." The butler lowers his head.

"I'll come at once."

William twists back around to face me. I can tell instantly that his anxiety is building.

"I'll come with you," I offer without hesitation.

"Thank you. You never know, I might need a lawyer."

"I'm sure it's nothing." I stand, and taking his hand, we follow the butler to the entrance of the house. I'm expecting plain clothes police officers, for some reason, but when I see they are in uniform, I can't help but feel even more uneasy.

"Hello," – William steps forward to greet the officers – "I'm William Cavendish, Earl Lullington. How may I help you?"

"Good afternoon, My Lord. We have a um... a delicate matter we need to discuss with you." The two uniformed officers, one male and one female, look toward me. The policewoman barely looks older than eighteen.

"This happens to be my lawyer, Miss Bennett. Anything you have to say to me can be said in front of her."

"Miss Bennett...Tamara Bennett?" the female officer questions.

"Yes," William answers.

"In that case, is there somewhere more comfortable we can talk?" The male officer jerks his head toward the door to the lounge. It's as though he's trying to tell William something, but I can't quite understand what.

"Officers, if there is an issue, could you tell us please? We are very busy today," William responds and folds his arms across his chest to signify he's not moving.

"My lord, as you wish," the male officer replies and turning to his colleague, he nods at her.

"Miss Bennett. I'm sorry to inform you that we were called to an incident earlier today in Kensington Park. On arrival, we found the body of a woman. She'd been attacked, raped and murdered. I'm sorry, Miss Bennett, but from the records we have, we believe the woman was your mother, Elsie Bennett."

The sound of the officer's words rushes through my ears like the wind of a gale. I'm not quite able to take them in before I feel myself falling to the hard marble floor. I never land, though, for I'm scooped into William's arms and seated on a nearby chaise longue.

"Bring brandy!" William shouts, and I'm unable to tell him I don't need it because no words can come out. My mother is dead. Beaten and raped. I don't need to be told who the culprit was because I already know – it was Viscount Hamilton.

"Have you arrested someone for the attack?" I come back to my senses. "Viscount Hamilton, do you have him in custody?"

"I'm sorry?" the male officer questions with confusion. "Viscount Hamilton? Her employer?"

"Yes. Do you have him in custody?" I ask again through gritted teeth.

"Miss Bennett, the Viscount was the person who found her and identified the body. He's terribly distraught. From all accounts, your mother was one of his favorite employees."

"So favorite that he raped her twenty-three years ago to conceive me. I want him arrested. Now!" I shout, and William tucks me under his arm.

"My apologies. I'm afraid Miss Bennett is distraught at this news."

"I'm not distraught." I push William away. "Give them the clothes and the letter. It's my mother's proof."

"Earl Lullington?" the male officer queries, pulling out his notebook to start writing details down. Finally, they're taking me seriously. He doesn't write, though. He reads from something already entered.

"Miss Bennett. We've already taken samples of DNA from your mother. Nothing, so far, matches with that of Viscount Hamilton. He volunteered to be tested himself just in case it would help."

"No." I shake my head at them. "No. You've got it wrong. I want to see her, please."

The officer nods.

"We'll take you to the morgue, at once."

I try to stand up, but my legs are too weak. William picks me up in his arms and carries me to the police car. I'm barely thinking straight, in fact, I'm barely functioning as we speed through the streets to my mother. My mother is dead – raped and murdered. I didn't want her to go back, but she did, and now she's dead. It's my fault. I should have stopped her. Why did we have to get mixed up in this secret society in the first place? I want my mother – I want to hear her voice, and I want to know she's alright and not suffering. But it doesn't matter what I want because it can't change anything. She must have suffered so much at the end. She was hurting and in pain, and I didn't know. I couldn't stop it, and I couldn't save her. I'm crying – my tears soak through William's shirt as he holds me closer to his chest. I vaguely register us arriving at our destination and him helping me out of the car. My legs are walking, but I'm not controlling them. I'm relying on William for support because I know I'll crumble if I let go. Doors are opening, people are talking around me, but I'm not taking anything in. Nothing registers in my numb brain until I see her. She's so tiny, my mother, the only person who's ever loved me unconditionally. She's lying on a silver table with a white sheet pulled up to her neck. Her face is covered in bruises, and her lips are swollen. Her eyes are shut, and she's pale, so very pale, like a ghost, but then I suppose that's what she is now: a spirit in the ether. I can only hope she comes back to haunt Viscount Hamilton, tormenting him so much he jumps from the highest building.

"Mummy," I whisper. I want her to answer. I want her to open her eyes, but she doesn't. She's dead. She's really dead. Bringing my hand up to her cheek, I stroke it. There's still a little warmth to her flesh. "I'm sorry," I cry, the words coming out of me in ragged sobs. "I love you. I promise you I will end him."

I take one final look at my mother before returning to William who'd been waiting at the doorway to give me some time alone with her. His eyes are watery, and I know he's feeling the emotion of the situation. He wraps his arms around me, and I bury my head in his chest and allow the grief to come.

CHAPTER NINETEEN

WILLIAM

"How is she?" My brother pokes his head around the door to Tamara's bedroom and whispers quietly.

"Sleeping still. The doctor gave her a sedative," I reply and look down to where I still hold her hand, having done so for the last five hours. I helped her to change into her nightdress when we returned home from the morgue, and then I put her to bed where she's been ever since.

"He gave Victoria a mild one also. She was getting stressed, and it was affecting the baby's heartbeat. I've left her sleeping."

"It's going to be hard for them both to come to terms with this." My thumb strokes over Tamara's hand.

"I can't help but think I could have done something more to protect her. I should've had a team in place sooner." Nicholas looks tired, really tired. The guilt weighing heavily upon his shoulders. "I should've refused to allow her to go back in."

"It's not your fault. That's the one thing I've realized sitting here. Elsie was an amazing woman, and she's the reason both Tamara and Victoria have the strength they do. For her to have survived what she did that first time, and then to see her tormentor every day, knowing it's the best thing for her daughter and her daughter's half-sister, must've taken some considerable willpower. We could have banned her from returning to the Viscount, even locked her in a room, but she still would have found a way to go back. That's the sort of woman she is...was. She wanted to help Theodore." I look to where Tamara stirs and turns over in the bed to face the other way. "In her memory, we will make sure we do just that."

"Yes, we will," Nicholas responds as he pushes off from the door frame he's been leaning against. "Goodnight, Brother."

"Goodnight."

He disappears, and I'm left alone with my thoughts. They are sad and painful but defiant. I lean back in the chair, allowing my heavy eyelids to droop shut, and I fall asleep. I don't know for how long, but I'm woken by Tamara abruptly sitting up in the bed. She screams, and I know she's had a nightmare.

Bringing her into my arms, I hold her in silence while she cries. Eventually, the heartbroken sobs stop wracking her body, and she quietens in my embrace.

"William?" Her eyes flick up to mine.

"Yes?" I stroke her head as a gesture of comfort and strength.

Hi "I need to know what she felt." Tamara pulls away from me and sits on the bed with her knees tucked under her.

"What do you mean?"

"I want you to chase me...to make me run." She looks down at the bed and twists her hand in the crumpled sheets. "To take me against my will."

I leap off the bed in shock and disbelief.

"What?"

"Please."

"No." I turn my back to her, but she gets off the bed and presses her warm body to mine.

"Allow the monster out. Please, I need him."

"You don't know what you're asking of me. I could hurt you or worse." I shut my eyes, trying to block out what she's asking. I want to put my hands over my ears and shout out no until the madness goes away.

"I trust you."

"You shouldn't."

"But I do." Tamara rests her head against my back. I'm only wearing a t-shirt, and I can feel the tears she's still crying, soak into the cotton fabric. "You think your mind is dark. Well, my blood is jet black. If you're a monster, then I'm the devil's spawn. Give me what I need. You're the only person who can."

My entire body chills at her words. I know she's right. I know exactly what she needs because I feel every inch of it in my bones, and I want it as well.

Grabbing her hand tightly, I allow the walls I've built up, which hide my true nature to crumble. I stride quickly through the corridors of the house and out into the garden. Tamara follows behind me, her shorter legs running to keep up with my fast pace. We come to a halt at the edge of the patio area.

"Run," I order with an intonation so brutal she just stares at me open mouthed. "If you want this, then run. I *will* find you. If you don't, we go back up to the room and sleep until your grief no longer makes you insane."

"I don't think that will ever happen," she whimpers and looks out over the vast blackness that's beckoning to her.

"And I'll never change. This will always be in me. The tics and lack of filter are the autism. You showed me that my sexual needs are another part of who I am."

The moon appears from its hiding place behind a bank of thick clouds. It illuminates Tamara's eyes, and I see the need and desire within them. It takes my breath away.

"Just as mine are a part of me," she tells me before taking off across the lawn. I pause for a moment to wrap my head around what I'm about to do. I'm going to hunt down the woman fleeing into the shadows and take her brutally, without care for her wellbeing. I'm going to allow the monster I suppress to claw its way to the surface and take over my body, unleashing the side of me that made my father proud. The only difference is this is a game, not a way of life, and I have Tamara's consent. I might be a monster, but I'm not the monster my father was.

The realization slams into my chest, leaving me breathless, momentarily, but then I see a flash of the woman I need through the moonlight's glow. My legs carry me after her, and the thrill of the chase is exhilarating. I reach the body of trees that lead into a woodland on our property, and I know she's in here. It's somewhere we walked the other day, and she commented on how it felt like a sanctuary. She wants all her illusions of protection shattered.

"I know you're in here," I growl and step forward into the darkness. I allow my hearing to take over in place of my sight. A twig cracks off to my left, and as I turn toward the sound, she's standing there with her eyes full of fear. I no longer have mercy running through my veins. She takes off running, but it doesn't take me long to catch up, and wrapping my arms around her, I lift her up into the air. She's so small and delicate in my hands. I could break her so easily. She's swinging her legs, trying to kick out at me, so I pin her up face first against a tree with her back toward me

"You wanted a monster. Well, now you've got one. Remember this. You asked for it, you cunt."

My erection is hard in my trousers, and I grind it against her bottom. She's pleading with me to stop but at the same time moaning her urgent need. I use my body weight to hold her in place and allow my rough hands to trace under the hem of her nightdress. I bunch it up around her hips, and she shivers when the cool air of the night hits her sensitive flesh. I don't give her any warning of my next movement and treat her just like the slut she's pretending to be. I kick her legs apart and propel three thick fingers into her core. She screams at the violent intrusion.

"No." Her skin pimples at the cold but also with the sensation of need tumbling through her body. She's an enigma of contradictions, at the moment. Need, desire, fear, and terror all combined into one yearning vessel.

"You are going to take everything I give you." I twist my fingers and thrust them in and out of her. She's dripping wet and coats me in her essence.

Reaching behind herself, she claws at my arm with her perfectly manicured nails.

"Bitch." I suck in a breath and add a fourth finger to intensify the stretching she feels at her entrance. My movements become faster and faster as I fuck her with my hand. My dick strains against the zipper of my trousers, desperately wanting out. It needs to bury itself balls deep in her tight little pussy.

"Stop," she cries underneath me, but even I can tell it's halfhearted. The flush of heat over her skin, and the tightening of the walls of her pussy around my fingers, tell me she's on the verge of an orgasm. I pull my hand away, and she lets out a long wail at the loss.

Leaning into her, I trail my tongue up the side of her face.

"This isn't about you getting off. Sluts don't get to come unless I say so." I jerk my hips toward her, so my hard shaft pokes her. "Do you know what happens next?"

"Please..." The whimpers are coming thick and fast, now. "Please...please don't hurt me."

"Too late, this monster's never retreating now. It's all about claiming what's his. You're. Mine. Forever."

I bring the fingers I've just had inside her up to her mouth, and I dip one inside. I feel her start to test the power of her teeth against my digit, and in the darkness surrounding us, I give her an ultimatum.

"Bite it, and I'll take you in the ass."

Her teeth retract, and I pull my finger out of her mouth. Lowering my hands to my trousers, I unzip them and pull out my hard length. I stroke it a few times, smearing the pre-cum at the head over the entire length. I don't think I've ever been as hard as I am right now.

"You know what girls like you get?" I ask.

"No," she cries.

"Hard and fast."

Before she has a chance to realize what I'm doing, I've thrust forward, bottoming out within her. My dick is now shrouded by her heat, and my mind flips completely as the dark mist clouding my brain, wraps around both of us, entwining us together. Two figures, in the dead of night, taking what they need from each other. My hips buck wildly as I withdraw and slam hard back into her. She'll feel me there constantly for the next few days.

"Please!" Tamara's screaming, her voice hoarse with the tears she's shed and the crying out she's been doing since I captured her. I know her last vestiges of control are hanging on a knife's edge. She needs one more thing to send her flying. With my nose, I nudge the material of her nightdress to the side, and as I bite down on her shoulder, her pussy clenches tighter around my dick, and she explodes in my arms. A powerful orgasm causing her body to shudder and shake under me as my own orgasm bursts from my balls and out of my dick to coat her insides.

Eventually, we are both still with me inside her, and my teeth embedded in her shoulder. My dick jerks, occasionally, but we remain silent in the shadows of the trees while far off in the distance, a church clock strikes midnight.

Tamara's legs give way, and I slip out of her and take her gently down onto the ground to protect her from a bad fall. She turns in my arms to face me. Speckles of moonlight through the branches of the trees illuminate her face.

"Thank you." She shuts her eyes. All her tears drying up. "This isn't wrong." Her eyes open, again, and I see honesty and happiness in them. They are tired and still edged with the grief she feels, but contentment is there. "We both consented, and that is the difference. The darkness is a part of us both, and it won't ever disappear. We just needed to find the right person to share it with."

Leaning forward, I press a soft, almost too tender kiss to her lips.

"Monsters together."

"Forever."

CHAPTER TWENTY

TAMARA

The sheets are twisted around my legs, and I kick out to free them. The friction between my thighs causes me to moan with the pain I feel down there, and I shift carefully, knowing I'm going to feel tender for a few days. The bed next to me dips, and I open my eyes to see William.

"Water and painkillers. You'll need them."

I groan and close my eyes again. Memories of the day before flood back: my mother's death, seeing her body in the morgue so broken and bruised, and being chased and caught by William in the forests of the Oakfield estate. My shoulder hurts from where he sunk his teeth into the flesh there, and I'm not looking forward to peeing because my lady parts are so sore, even the flats of my feet feel torn apart.

"Why do you have to have such a big dick?" I pout, needing to distract myself from my mother's death. If I let the grief overwhelm me, I won't be able to channel the anger I have into destroying Viscount Hamilton.

"I was born with it." William chuckles, and I hear him place the water and tablets down before wrapping his arms around my shoulders and pulling me up in the bed.

"Ouch, ouch, ouch." I squirm and open my eyes to glare at him.

"Stop being a baby." He opens my mouth, pops the tablets in, and hands me the water to help swallow.

"A baby!" I cough as one of them gets stuck in my throat. I hate taking medicine.

"Yes." He raises his eyebrow.

"You want me to tell Victoria you called me that?" I retort with a smug smirk on my face. "I swear she's going to go after your balls today. I can't believe she saw you carrying me back to my room!"

William grumbles and gets to his feet to take a sip from a cup of a coffee he must have brought for himself along with the water for me.

"I'll get Nicholas to give her stronger sedatives next time. I like my balls where they are."

I laugh and then realize the words he chose.

"There will be a next time?"

William stops drinking midway with his cup to his mouth. He places it down on my bedside table and climbs into the bed with me. He shifts me effortlessly, like a rag doll to his needs, so I'm sitting across his lap. Part of me likes it, but part of me wishes he wasn't all toned and muscular. I need a softer cushion similar to the memory foam mattress I've been sleeping on. He must sense my discomfort and tucks me into his side instead.

"Do you want another time?"

"Not right now, but yes."

"Ok, we'll do it again, but no sex for you until your fully healed. I'll just have to stick my dick in your mouth for now."

I must stare at him blankly because a mischievous smirk crosses his face.

"Only if we both agree and consent," I retort as he kisses the tip of my nose and says,

"Always."

I lean into his chest, listening to the beat of his heart.

"How are you feeling?" William questions and fresh tears prick in my eyes. I shouldn't be this happy when I have my mother's funeral to arrange.

"Numb, I think. I'm happy I'm here with you, but I still can't believe she's gone. My mother, my beautiful, wonderful, caring Mummy. I'll never get to speak to her again. Who will I ask for advice?"

"She'll still be there for you if you need her."

"How?"

"Something my brother told me when our mother died. I was upset because I needed her, having fallen over and scraped my knee. I cried for her to help me. My father got frustrated and stormed off, but Nicholas kneeled down next to me and told me that if I ever needed my mother, I just had to talk to her. She was an angel and although I'd never get to see her again, she was always there for me because angels were allowed to walk the Earth to help those they love. I stifled my tears and started talking out loud, asking her to take the pain away. It may have been the wind, but I'm almost certain I felt her blow on my knee, and it immediately stopped hurting."

"That's beautiful. I've always believed something similar. I'll miss her every day." My voice cracks, and William squeezes me a little tighter to him. "But I know she's here with me."

"Just not when we're having sex," William adds.

I can't help but let laughter engulf me. It's needed.

"What?" William huffs, not realizing the bluntness of his words. "That's just a no-no."

"I promise. My mother will shut her eyes when we're having sex."

I pull myself up from his chest, so I can bring my lips to his.

"Tamara."

Victoria's hammering on my bedroom door while at the same time she's shouting in a shrill voice.

"Are you decent? I'm coming in."

William jumps up off the bed and stands beside it with his hand cupped hard over his manhood.

"She's not getting my balls."

"Victoria, I said you're not going." Nicholas' stern tones come through the door next.

"Fuck you," Victoria responds and without waiting for me to invite her in, she opens the door and storms in. She grabs my discarded jeans and jumper from the previous day and throws them at me.

"Put them on."

"Victoria, I said no." Nicholas grabs her arm while trying to reason with her.

"And I told you to fuck off with the rules and regulations. I don't give a shit about them, right now. All I care about is seeing him arrested," Victoria adamantly spits words at her husband.

"She consented," William mutters from the other side of the bed to the warring husband and wife.

"What?" Victoria turns toward her brother-in-law and screws her tiny little nose up in confusion.

"Tamara consented. It was mutual between us. You can't have me arrested," William protests his case, and I open my mouth to agree with him.

Victoria shakes her head, though, "I'm not having you arrested, you great lummox. Whatever you did to Tamara left her with the same goofy look on her face Nicholas gets after I suck his dick. I knew she was happy and had consented. No, this is about my father. Our father."

I shuffle gingerly forward in the bed.

"What about him?"

"I don't know all the details, but the police are going to bring him in for questioning." Victoria makes a hurrying motion with her hands, and I pull my jumper on over the clean nightdress William put me in last night.

"On what charges? My mother's murder?"

"We don't know," Nicholas replies and quickly turns around to give me privacy when Victoria pulls the covers away from the lower half of my body. "All I know is that the police are on the way to bring him in for questioning on a matter of importance. The fact they are going to collect him and not allow him to surrender himself at a police station, suggests it's likely to be for a criminal offense of a serious nature."

"Yes, it will be." I hold my breath, not daring to believe that maybe the Viscount actually made a mistake when he killed my mother and will be charged with her murder.

"Do we have my mother's letter and DNA evidence? We might need to present it to strengthen the case."

"It's in safekeeping. If it comes to it, I'll make sure it finds its way into police hands," Nicholas confirms.

"Put some shoes on," Victoria interrupts. "We don't have much time, and I don't want to miss this."

"Miss what?" William asks the question also on my mind.

"Duh!" Victoria rolls her eyes and throws my trainers at me, narrowly missing my head. "Seeing my father get arrested. We're going to Hamilton Manor. I wouldn't miss this for the world."

"No, you aren't," Nicholas grinds out through clenched teeth.

"Again, husband dearest, fuck you." Victoria smiles at him, and Nicholas raises an eyebrow at her, daring her to test him further. "I'm not missing this. I deserve it for all the years he closeted me away like a hermit, then sacrificed me without a second thought."

"He gave you to me?" Nicholas reminds her of how they came to find love.

"No, he gave me away for his advancement in the society."

"I think we should go," William adds. He's already slipping his feet into a pair of socks and shoes. "If Viscount Hamilton's getting arrested, I want to see it as well."

"I want to go too." I say, pulling on my trainers.

Nicholas throws his hands up in the air.

"Am I the only one with any sanity?" He shakes his head and stomps back toward the door. "I'll call for the car."

The journey to Victoria's and my childhood home is completed in tense silence. All of us willing the car to go quicker, so we can witness Viscount Hamilton being arrested. When we pull up the driveway, there are several other cars already parked. Some are marked police cars, and the others, I suspect, are unmarked ones.

William helps me out of the car at the same time as Theodore descends the steps of the manor house with a smartly dressed older man.

"A lawyer, just what my father needs," Theodore addresses me while shooting daggers toward William and Nicholas.

"Will this be your father's defense barrister?" The smartly dressed man asks. "I'm Detective Inspector French."

"No," I reply instantly. "Prosecution, maybe, but it'll be a cold day in hell before I'll defend him on any charges."

"Have they taken him yet?" Victoria asks her brother. I know she's nervous to see the man who gave her away like a chattel, but she holds herself upright with all the decorum of her new position as the Duchess of Oakfield.

Theodore shakes his head. "I don't know what hold they have over you, Victoria, and you Tamara, but whatever it is has gone too far. False allegations against our father of tax avoidance. It's ludicrous."

"Tax avoidance?" Victoria and I both say at the same time.

"But what about murdering my mother?" I step forward, and the detective motions to some of the uniformed officers to be prepared in case things turn nasty.

"Murder?" Theodore exclaims with utter indignation.

"You want criminals, Detective? Then look no further than the Cavendish brothers. They are guilty of brainwashing, abuse, and god knows what else. They've turned perfectly intelligent women into lunatics. My father did not kill your mother. You want a culprit then, maybe, look closer to home."

"He raped her. I'm your sister," I spit at him.

"Detective, I want these people off my property."

"It's just as much my property as it is yours," Victoria counters.

"No it's not, Sister. Our father has more intelligence than the lot of you put together. He knew something like this would happen, so he signed everything over to me. Right before he disappeared."

"Disappeared?" I feel my legs wobble, and William is there behind me, holding me up.

"Yes. I've not seen him since the night your mother was murdered. He's been threatened by the Cavendish brothers for some time now. I know they killed their own father to take over the title, and I'll not stop until I see them rotting in jail for what they've done. Now, I want you off my property. All of you."

Theodore storms back up the steps of Hamilton Manor and slams the front door firmly shut behind him. The police officers give us funny looks and start to mill back toward their cars – all but the senior detective.

"Interesting," he says, rubbing his beard and resting a hand over his rotund stomach.

"I think I might have a new case to investigate besides the one against Viscount Hamilton." He bows his head, recognizing Nicholas' status as the Duke. "Your Grace, Earl Lullington, I'm sure this won't be the last you'll see me, assuming Lord Hamilton's accusations are true. If this young lady is a lawyer, you might want to start working with her on your defenses."

As the detective walks away, Victoria slides down onto the steps leading up to our hated former home. Defeat is written all over her face.

"He's got away with it," I announce– almost in a dreamlike state.

William pulls me into him.

"Not yet. He may have won this round, but I'm not stopping now. That's one of the good things about autistic people. Once we get a hard-on for something, we don't give up on it easily."

CHAPTER TWENTY-ONE

WILLIAM

*"And now to him who is able to keep us from falling,
and lift us from the dark valley of despair
to the bright mountain of hope,
from the midnight of desperation
to the daybreak of joy;
to him be power and authority, for ever and ever.
Amen."*

Tamara picks up a handful of soil from the ground and follows the priest by throwing it on top of her mother's coffin. She leans back into me as Victoria does the same with her little piece of earth. We say goodbye one final time and turn away, back to Oakfield Hall. There was, initially, some debate as to where Tamara's mother should be buried until Nicholas suggested she could have the vacant plot next to our mother – the one my father should've had his body buried in when he died. Instead, we'd had his body cremated, and we'd flushed the contents of the urn down the toilet. It seemed a really fitting tribute to the woman who was considered to be not only a surrogate mother to the current Duchess of Oakfield, but also the actual mother of the woman for whom my feelings are increasing in intensity the more time I spend in her company.

Tamara's fragile, at the moment, and we have good days and bad together. She's frustrated that Viscount Hamilton disappeared as are Nicholas, Victoria, and I. But we all know we can't let this set-back stop our ultimate goal, which is to destroy all that remains of the previous Oakfield Society. It will happen – along with the downfall of Viscount Hamilton. It's just going to take a while longer than we expected.

"Anyone want a drink?" Nicholas asks as we enter the lounge.

"Please," I reply and escort Tamara over to the sofa. Victoria takes a seat on the high-backed armchair she's taken a preference to, and Nicholas tucks a blanket over her lap to keep her warm before going to prepare three brandies. He calls down to the kitchen to request hot chocolate for Victoria.

"To Ms. Elsie Bennett" – he raises his cup when we all have drinks in hand – "a woman whose courage and fortitude knew no bounds. I'll be forever grateful to her for imparting some of that to my beautiful wife. Even if she uses it to bust my balls on occasion."

Victoria snorts a wry smile and holds her hot chocolate up.

"To my nanny and surrogate mother. I'll miss you every day, but I'll make sure this little one"–she runs her empty hand over her stomach– "knows all about you. Thank you."

I hold my glass up next. I don't have much to say, just a few words. "Thank you for giving me Tamara. She really is your greatest gift. I promise I'll protect her for you."

Tamara stares blankly into her brandy, and we all wait for her to find the words she wants to say.

She pushes up onto her feet.

"I could rant and rave and say I'll avenge your death. That I won't rest until the Viscount is rotting behind bars or better yet dismembered and rotting in the ground, but I'm not going to. I'm just going to share my first memory of you." She shuts her eyes and licks her lips to steady herself. As always, I'm close to her, ready to catch her should she fall. "My greatest time spent with you was always in the kitchens. I don't know how you stood to be in them after what happened to you there, but I guess I gave you new memories, ones to replace the horror. I always remember the day you tried to teach me how to prepare the meal your father had taught you. His mother's recipe for pineapple sandwiches. You took the bread and placed on to it a slice of ham and one of those round rings of pineapple from a can. We then smothered it in cheese and put it under the grill until all the cheese was melted. The chef was a stuck-up bastard, and he was horrified we were preparing such mundane food in his kitchen, but I loved it. My favorite meal in the world." She laughs, but it catches in her throat, turning into a sob. "Always. I'll always be your daughter, and he will die for what he did." Bringing the brandy glass up to her mouth, she drinks the burning nectar down in one long steady gulp before placing the empty glass back down onto the table in front of her.

"William, I'm tired. Will you come sleep with me for a while?"

She looks straight at me, and I know we'll be doing anything but sleeping when we go to our bedroom. It's what she needs, though, and who am I to deny my woman? I've been doing a lot of thinking over the last few days. I've put a halt on my acceptance at the autistic home, mainly because Tamara can't join me there and the thought of being away from her breaks me out in a cold sweat. I've also come to realize it's not my autism causing the darkness within me – it's the result of my upbringing, and my father's influence. However, it's also something a part of me enjoys. The difference is now I can control it, and I know I won't murder or destroy a woman just because I can. I'll always have oddities because my brain is wired differently, but Tamara brings the best out in me. I was locked away for so many years, and although the world outside of Oakfield Hall is terrifying as hell, I want to see it. I want to go on a plane, a boat, even a train – experience things I never have before. I'm not sure about having to queue to do it, but I want to try. I want to be as normal as I can. That's what the children at the day care center had, and it showed me I could have it too. A warm feeling settles in my chest, but it's swiftly replaced by a swelling in my groin when Tamara winks at me.

"Of course." Taking her hand, I lead her to my bedroom.

"Is this wrong?" she asks as our lips meet, and I'm ripping her smart, black suit from her body.

"Do you want it?"

"Yes," she whispers breathlessly. "I need to feel. I want to lose myself in your taste and touch, so I don't have to think."

I step back from her. I've totally destroyed her clothes, and she's standing before me in a black bra and matching thong.

Fuck, she's sexy as hell. Part of me feels it's wrong to be doing this so soon after burying her mother, but I know Tamara needs it. She needs to forget in order to start living and breathing again, and this is the only way. We've not done anything since the night in the forest – just spent our nights together in each other's arms.

I allow my monster to take over, and as I transition, I realize, for the first time, that even as a monster I'm still the same person because it's who I am. I like the wild side. I pick a cushion up off the chair beside me and drop it onto the floor at my feet.

"On your knees," I order, and Tamara licks her lips.

I unbuckle my suit trousers, pull down the zipper, and lower them along with my underpants to my feet. Tamara kneels in front of my dick as it springs out, ready for her succulent little mouth to wrap itself around it. As a couple, we are a contradiction in terms. Sometimes she's bossy and looks after me, and sometimes it's the other way around. But here in the bedroom, I'm always in control, and I couldn't give a fuck if anyone says I'm weak because I let her rule me elsewhere. They aren't about to get their dick sucked by the hottest woman in the world.

"Open," I demand, and she does so without question. "I've been on edge for a few days. My poor dick, spending its night lying next to that pussy of yours but not being able to get inside. I'm going to take your mouth. Claim it. I won't be gentle. I'll make you gag, but you'll take every inch of me."

Fuck, I nearly shoot my load, there and then, when she circles her tongue around her partially open lips in anticipation.

I stroke up and down my length a few times before pushing it in between her plump, pink lips. Her mouth is wet and warm with the still lingering effect of the brandy, caressing me with its heat. I push all the way in until I hit the back of her throat, and she gags. Damn, it's beautiful. Her eyes widen when she realizes I really won't take this easy on her. I pull my hips back and slam back in again.

"This is my hole to fuck. I'm going to do so while you swallow me deep until I come down your throat."

I allow the speed of my hips to increase and wrap her hair around my hand, so I can keep her head still. Saliva pools in Tamara's mouth as she remains helpless to the onslaught. I piston in and out of her mouth like a jackhammer. Her eyes water and tears fall from them, but they're not the same as the ones she shed earlier. These are tears of a woman being taken and worshipped by her man. I know I won't last long, because this feeling is just too good. Tamara tries to swirl her tongue around my dick as I push in and out, but I'm wide in girth, and there's too little room for her to do anything other than take what I give. Her hands come up and rest on my taut thighs, but she applies no pressure to stop me. It's merely to steady herself. My balls draw up, and I know the end is near for me. I want to stop time in this very moment and remember it forever. Once I've emptied myself, I plan on ensuring Tamara is pleasured and will be walking with a strange gait tomorrow. My orgasm races up through my shaft, and I bury myself deep inside Tamara's mouth and throat. I hold her head so tightly the roots of her hair must be burning with pain as I come with a loud moan of her name. Spurt after spurt of my cum shoots down her throat, which is working overtime to swallow everything, including my dick that's so far down it's constricting her breathing. After what feels like an eternity, probably for both of us, I pull out, and she collapses on the ground, breathing air into her parched lungs. My dick doesn't soften – it wants more.

"I'm not finished yet." I grab her and throw her onto the bed, and in one swift movement, I'm inside her pussy. "Not at all. I plan on spending the next few hours in my cunt. Reminding it that it's mine. You wanted the monster in me, Tamara, and now you've got him because he's fallen in love with you."

She gasps at my words, and I pause in my thrusts.

"Love?" she breathlessly utters.

"Love," I reply, not needing to hear it from her if she isn't ready to give me the actual words yet. The way her pussy is already clenching around my dick tells me all I need to know, for now.

CHAPTER TWENTY-TWO

TAMARA

"I won't be long. I'm just going to drop these papers off at court, and then I'll be back. You stay in bed… keep it warm for when I return." I lean in to kiss a sleepy William's lips as he lies in the bed we've shared every night since my mother's funeral, almost two months ago. He was up late last night, returning another one of the art pieces the society had stolen. It's the last one to be returned, for now. The rest have been hidden away deep in the Oakfield vault and are likely to remain there for some time, yet. It's a shame the valuable pieces won't be seen, but the risk to Nicholas and William from their breaking and entering is becoming too much. Security is tighter, and if they are caught, it is highly unlikely I'd be able to get a custodial sentence of anything less than twenty to thirty years for them both. It's a life time, and one Victoria and I are not prepared to spend without them.

"Don't go alone," William murmurs as his eyes drift shut again.

"I won't. I've got one of Nicholas' bodyguards coming with me."

"Good." He turns over in the bed and before long is softly snoring again. I made a spur-of-the-moment decision to do this, last night, while I was finishing the documentation I needed, and I managed to get an appointment with a judge I admire. I haven't actually spoken to Nicholas, but I have spoken to his driver who'll sort it all out for me. I stop, for a few moments, and watch William – I've been so lucky to find him. We are both very different from each other, but that's what makes us so strong together. Sometimes he's the controlling one, and sometimes, maybe, I am. It allows us both to get exactly what we need from our relationship, and it's only going from strength to strength. Between my thigh's throbs at the thought of the heights of ecstasy he can bring me to. I think maybe later I'll ask him to chase me through the forest again – I want it rough and dirty tonight. I can't get enough.

I reach for my Mulberry briefcase, sitting ready on the top of the sideboard, and place it over my shoulder. I open the heavy oak door to the bedroom, quietly, hoping it doesn't squeak on its antique hinges and wake William again. I breathe a sigh of relief when I'm out of the room, and I take the stairs down to the front door at a skip. The driver's waiting in the hallway for me.

"Good morning, Miss Bennett." He bows his head at me out of courtesy.

"Good morning," I reply.

"I've had the car running to warm it up. It's below zero out there at the moment. I think we could get snow later."

"I bet the Oakfield grounds are pretty when it snows."

"They are. I remember the current Duke and Earl running around and building snowmen as boys. It was good to see."

"You've worked here a long time, then."

I place my bag on the ground, and he hands me a thick overcoat to put on while he collects my bag and then waits for me to finish doing up the buttons on the coat.

"Almost thirty years."

"You don't look old enough."

"I don't know. Days when the wind is this cold, I certainly feel it." The driver laughs as he opens the front door and escorts me to the waiting car where I slide into the back seat. It's lovely and warm when I get in, and I immediately start to undo my coat.

"That's the thing I hate about this weather. It's on and off with coats all the time."

"Tell me about it." He removes his thick jacket and places it on the passenger seat. The car pulls away before I have a chance to register that we don't have one of Nicholas' guards in the vehicle with us.

"Aren't we supposed to have a bodyguard with us?" I lean forward and query.

"In the vehicle behind." The driver looks in the mirror, and I turn my head to see a black Range Rover following us.

"Good."

I settle back into my car for the journey into London. I'm going straight to the highest authority with the papers I want signing, and then I'm meeting with a friend of mine at the criminal courts in the Old Bailey. Opening my bag, I pull out the sheets of paper to check them one final time. I become engrossed in the information, knowing the contents will help to freeze the assets of some of the key conspirators within the society who still want it to be run the old-fashioned way. It's not going to happen. Once these are filed, Nicholas and William will be fully in control of the new Oakfield Society and can start to run it the way they want. We spent the other night discussing ideas, and they have so many great ones. The Oakfield Society will become synonymous with helping people, especially woman. Not destroying them.

When I look up from my papers, I expect to see the sights of London around me, but I don't. It's still countryside.

"Are we going a different way?" I ask the driver, but he doesn't reply. He simply flicks a switch on the dashboard, and all the doors lock around me. The skin on the back of my neck pricks, and I know I'm in trouble. I reach into my bag and look for my phone but it's not there. I'm certain I put it in there this morning – I remember doing it. "Please, stop the car," I say to the driver, but he doesn't reply. He puts his foot down, and we go a little faster. I lean forward, again, and see my phone in a compartment between the two front seats. He must have taken it out of my bag. I make a grab for it, but he's quicker.

"Sit down, Miss Bennett," he orders.

"What are you doing?"

"Making sure you don't destroy what I spent most of my life working hard to help build."

I turn around in my seat and start to wave at the vehicle behind us, containing the bodyguard. The driver laughs, an eerie cackle, which brings bile to my throat.

"Wave all you want. They aren't Nicholas' bodyguards. They're helping me bring you in to him."

"Him?" I question but don't get a response. "Turn this car

around and take me back to Oakfield Hall. I will see the brothers pay you handsomely to disappear. You won't get into any trouble from whoever is paying you to take me."

"Do you think I'm stupid? The brothers will kill me and drop my body parts around the country as a warning to others. No. It's going to be your parts delivered, not mine."

The car turns left, and we drive up what looks like a deserted road at the end of which is a small house. Trying to stay calm, I think of what I need to do and look for ways to escape, but my stomach is tied in knots. I'm struggling with the emotions flooding through me because all I can think is...Will I see my father when the doors to the house open? Is he the one who's come for me? I don't think I'm ready to face him, yet. I can't. I can't know what he did to my mother. I shut my eyes and whisper in my head for William. I know he can't hear me, but I want to believe he can.

The car comes to a halt, and the driver unlocks the doors. I make the split-second decision I need to run for it, and thrusting the door open, I'm out of the car and running as fast as my legs can take me. I wish it was William chasing me and this was a game, but I know it isn't. Men shout behind me, and footsteps thunder in pursuit. I don't know how I'm keeping in front of them. It's sheer determination. I can see the road, and I know there were houses as we pulled in. If I can make it to one of them, I'll be safe. I will my legs to propel me faster, and they do. I lost my smart shoes ages ago, and I'm now running bare foot. I can see a house – it's there in front of me, my sanctuary, my safety. I'm going to make it, but a hand wraps around my waist, and I'm hoisted backward. I go to scream, but another hand slams over my mouth. No. No! I'm dragged back toward where the car is parked as my sanctuary disappears into the horizon. My legs kick furiously, connecting with solid matter, and I sink my teeth into the hand over my mouth.

"Fucking bitch!" a man shouts, and he drops me to the ground. I'm pushing myself up ready to run again, but he kicks me in the stomach with his heavy snow boot so hard all the air is expelled from me. A fist meets my face, and the pain shatters through me. The fist connects again, and then the boot repeats its action only this time higher and in my ribs. I hear them crack.

"Enough," an authoritative voice orders.

"The bitch drew blood," the man who'd been hitting me protests.

"And I'll give you time with her to punish her, later. First, we have business to conduct, and I need her as conscious as possible for that."

My head is spinning from the assault, but I try to focus on where the commanding voice is coming from. Is it my father? I can't distinguish the inflections, because of the ringing in my ear.

"Get her inside. Remove her clothes and strap her up. It's time for me to have fun and destroy the Cavendish brothers, forever."

I'm lifted up, my head flopping uncontrollably as I try to maintain consciousness. Behind me, I see figures as I'm carried like a rag doll into the house, but everything is blurry. I can't see who gives the orders, a flash of blue swipes in front of my face and words flood into my ears.

"Don't worry, Tamara. I'll make this as painful for you as possible."

It's then I realize who holds me, and I know I won't make it out alive.

CHAPTER TWENTY-THREE

WILLIAM

"Are you getting up today, you lazy ass?" My brother throws a pillow at my head, and I reach out, grab it, and hurl it back at him.

"Sleeping," I groan

"It's two o'clock in the afternoon!"

That wakes me up.

"What?"

"You sleep any longer, and you won't sleep tonight."

"Thanks, Mum!" I roll my eyes at my brother and sit up in the bed.

"Where's Tamara? She was supposed to wake me up when she got back from court."

"Court?" my brother asks, his brows crossed in confusion.

"Yeah. You gave her a bodyguard to take with her."

"No. I wasn't aware she was going anywhere. I've been with Victoria all morning. She's so bloody horny all the time I think my dick's getting chafed." Nicholas smiles smugly.

"She told me you gave her a bodyguard."

"Did you dream it? You do sometimes get confused." The tension in the room thickens as we both try to make sense of where Tamara is.

"No. She definitely told me that. I'm sure." I reach over to the night stand and pick up my mobile. Using the fingerprint reader, I open it and call Tamara. It rings and rings before going to voicemail. I try again, but there's still no answer.

"Get up, and we'll go search the house. I'm sure she's here, somewhere. Probably working away and paying no attention to the phone."

"Ok." Nicholas turns around to allow me to get out of the bed and put some clothes on. I throw on a pair of jogging bottoms and a t-shirt from yesterday. I'll worry about being clean later when I know where Tamara is. My mind is confused, and I can't fully understand what's happening. Tiredness and overstimulation are combining to make me forgetful. I'm trying to focus, but it's not possible at the moment.

"We'll find her." Nicholas must sense my worry, for he places his hand on my shoulder. "I'll check the house. You go down to her mother's grave and see if she's there."

The short walk to where Tamara's mother and my mother lie side by side, seems to take an eternity. I know instantly she's not there and hasn't been recently because a light covering of snow has fallen on the ground, and there are no footprints. I stand between the two graves and place my hands on top of them.

"Look after her, wherever she is."

I head back to the house, kick my boots off by the patio doors, and remain standing there when I see Victoria sitting on the sofa, chewing nervously at her nails.

"Was she there?"

I shake my head. Nicholas appears, and worry lines mar his face.

"Did you find her?"

"No, and my driver is also missing. The butler said Tamara left with him early this morning. He didn't know where they were going. If he did, he would have informed one of us immediately."

"Oh god." Victoria covers her mouth with her hand.

Nicholas takes his mobile from the table, next to where Victoria sits, and dials a number. He puts the phone on speaker while it rings, but it goes to the driver's voicemail.

"Try Tamara's again?" he suggests with trepidation lacing his normally calm tones.

I pull my phone from my pocket and call Tamara with bated breath. I will her to answer, but when it goes to voicemail, I gulp and try to moisten my rapidly drying throat. Something is wrong… seriously wrong.

"Would she have her phone turned off if she's in court?" Victoria asks, trying to find a reason for her not answering.

"Maybe, but my driver wouldn't. He's expected to always answer his phone. If he doesn't, he's fired. It's in the contract my father made him sign, and I've not renegotiated it yet." Nicholas' response burns down that theory. "I'm going to call in some people I know, see if we can get a track on her phone."

He starts typing a short message into his phone while Victoria and I both watch him. My hand comes up to my head and swipes across my ear then my nose. I'm anxious, and that does nothing for the mis-wiring in my head. My other hand forms a fist then relaxes before forming a fist again.

"She's tough. We'll find her." Victoria appears beside me, leaning in to give me comfort, and I wrap my arm around her shoulders. Nicholas looks up from his phone, and his face immediately goes white as a sheet.

"Move!" he shouts, and he's running for us just as the wall and door behind us explode in a hail of glass and bricks. I can't believe what I'm seeing when a car comes speeding in. I grab Victoria and throw her out of the way toward Nicholas and dive sideways, managing to narrowly avoid being hit as the car slams to a halt in the center of our lounge.

"Nicholas." I'm on my feet and coughing due to the debris and dust in the room. I hear another masculine cough, and Nicholas gets to his feet. The butler and some of the other staff run into the room.

"Ok," Nicholas informs me.

"Victoria?"

"Safe," she replies, but I know from the blood dripping down the side of her head she's not uninjured. She places her hand on her stomach and groans.

"Get me a doctor," Nicholas shrieks, and people start running around like crazy.

"I'm ok." Victoria says as her legs give way. Nicholas sweeps her up, and we hurriedly leave the room. I think I pulled something in my left leg when I leaped out of the way of the moving car because I'm limping, and my calf muscle is painful.

Nicholas puts Victoria down in the hallway. He's examining her body.

"The baby?" he asks.

"Ok. It's kicking. I think it's angry," Victoria reassures him.

"Thank god."

He tilts her head back and scrutinizes the cut on her forehead. "It doesn't look too bad. I'll get the doctor to look at it."

He motions to one of the maids.

"Take the Duchess to her room, help her change, and then put her to bed."

"Nicholas, I'm not a child. We need to find Tamara."

"No arguments. You've got our child in there, and if it's kicking you because it's angry, you need to rest to placate it."

"Seriously?"

"Yes."

"Ok. Keep me informed of everything, though."

"I will." Victoria kisses her husband and disappears up the stairs with the maid who's supporting her on her unsteady legs.

"You ok?" Nicholas asks me and nods down to where I'm flexing my painful leg.

"Yes. I think I pulled something," I reply and perform a calf stretch.

"It didn't hit you?"

"No. Narrowly missed. What the fuck, though?" I look into the room where the dust still billows out.

"My thoughts exactly. I better call the police." Nicholas rubs his dusty hand over his head and hair, leaving it with a grey sheen.

The door to the lounge opens, and the butler comes out. We don't need him to speak to know something is seriously wrong and not just because there's a car sitting pride of place in the lounge where our sofa once was.

"Your Grace, I think you need to see this before you call the authorities."

Nicholas and I file into the room behind the butler. We make our way over the discarded bricks, being careful not to catch ourselves on shards of glass. The dust is starting to settle but is likely to linger in the air for a long time to come. My cough is triggered again.

We step nearer to the car, and I see instantly through the smashed glass of the windscreen why the butler was so worried. The body of our dead driver sits there with the word traitor carved into his forehead. Half of his skull is missing where it's obviously been shot away by a gun. I'm looking behind him for Tamara, but the back seat is empty except for her phone.

"Do you hear noise?" Nicholas questions, and I listen carefully. I can hear voices, and they're coming from Tamara's phone. I reach into the vehicle carefully and retrieve it.

"Hello?" I speak into it.

"About time." A deep toned voice I instantly recognize comes through, and the phone beeps. I pull it away from my ear and note a request for a FaceTime call. My finger trembles as I press it. Tamara's face appears on the screen. It's bruised and blood drips from her lip. The phone camera pulls away, and I see she's naked and tied to a bed. Her arms and legs are secured by chains.

"What have you done?" I ask with my voice quivering.

"Nothing yet. I hope you like my little gift. Your driver was so easy to manipulate, you need to watch your staff better. I gave him the send-off a traitor deserves though. Can't have him reporting this to the police, now, can we?" The phone swings away from Tamara and onto the face of my old companion. The man who I've shared women with, Lord West.

"But you know exactly what I'm capable of. I warned you both. I told you to leave me alone. Now, I'll force you to."

He turns the phone back to Tamara, and I watch as a bucket of water is thrown over her to revive her. She screams out with wild eyes when she realizes what's happening. The caller hangs up before I'm able to speak to her.

Nicholas takes the phone from my hands.

"William?"

I don't hear him, though, as I allow the darkness in my mind free rein. Lord West wants the monster. He's going to get him!

CHAPTER TWENTY-FOUR

TAMARA

The water splashes into my face, and I'm brought completely back to my senses by the icy coldness of it. My ribs ache, and my face feels like I've gone ten rounds with Mike Tyson.

"Welcome, Tamara. You've just missed William. I gave him a call just to show him how lovely you look when tied to my bed. I'm sure he'll be busy trying to find out where you are at the moment. Shame nobody knows I have this place. It's my sanctuary from the outside world – the place I can be myself." Lord West runs his foul hand over my body while talking to me. I want to jerk away and stop him, but I'm tied down so tightly I can't move. I take a moment to scope out where I am. It appears to be a small room, sparsely decorated with rich red walls that have candle lamps hanging from them, giving a dim light. The place has a feeling of being old, a place of torment from a bygone time. There are two other men in the room. I recognize one as the guard who captured me when I ran, but the other is the face of a stranger. I half expected it to be the driver. I guess he doesn't get to see through his plan to destroy the Cavendish brother's now he's brought me here.

"You're a sick freak." I let the words escape from my mouth before my brain engages, and I know the instant they leave I'll regret them.

"Not a good thing to say to the man who now owns every part of you until I tire of it. That's the thing about the original Oakfield Society: it puts women in their rightful place, not like these modern feminist movements, trying to empower women and making men weak in the process. You should be home ready and willing, for when your master demands it. Women are made for sex. Why else would you have holes and us the staffs to punish you with? Women have become less humble and more stupid as the years have gone by. We need to return things to how they used to be by reinstalling discipline. This is what Nicholas doesn't understand. He allows his wife to wear his balls around her neck like a trophy, celebrating his downfall."

"Whereas, you just wear yours as a sign of how small your dick is?" I just couldn't stop myself saying it.

"You'll soon find *that* to be far from the truth. It's a shame you were still sleeping when I spoke to William. He could have confirmed the damage I can do with just one thrust. He's been there cheering me on before with his dick in hand because, let's face it, nobody wants a freak near them. Even if he's the Duke's brother."

Lord West is still trailing his hands over my body. I'm going to need a damn good shower with bleach after this.

"I always find those who are all talk have little going on for them down there." I muse into the air. I know I should be frightened, but to be honest, I'm more pissed off because even if I get out of this alive, I'm going to be ruined for William. Maybe he was right, and we are freaks together. A situation that should leave me a quivering wreck is making me angry. Go figure!

"Whatever you're planning on doing can you just get on with it. No wonder William had to take matters into his own hands. You like to hog all the attention."

Lord West looks down at me.

"My god, it's not a disguise is it? You really aren't scared of what I can do to you."

"Nope." I roll my eyes.

"Wow. I've never had that happen before. There's always fear from the underlying threat of what I can do. It leaves a glimmer of doubt in a girl's eyes even when they try to disguise it. I don't know – it feels strange." He reaches into his trousers and re-arranges himself. "You have a pussy, though. Screaming or not. I can still rip it in two."

He takes his hand from his trousers. My legs are parted on the bed with my most intimate parts freshly shaven and bared to him. My pussy is William's property, but that doesn't stop Lord West from taking two of his filthy fingers and pushing them straight into me. I'm dry, and they rip at the sensitive flesh. There is no pleasure, just pain, and the promise of retribution. He thrusts hard, trying to illicit a scream from me, but I will not give it up. If he wants me begging for mercy, he's going to have to try harder.

"You do realize who I am don't you?" I sneer at him when he withdraws his fingers and licks them.

"A frigid little bitch?" he retorts with amusement at his choice of words.

"Hardly. I'm Viscount Hamilton's illegitimate daughter."

"What?" That piece of information stops him in his tracks. "You can't be."

"Why not? Isn't he the same sort of bastard as you are? A rapist and murderer? I always wondered why I didn't have a father, never realizing he was there all along. He just couldn't say because he knew I'd hate him for the way he treated my mother."

"More like he made a mistake. If you get them pregnant, you put a bullet in their brain before they have a chance to spawn a bastard. Nobody in our position needs that."

I gather as much salvia as I can in my dry mouth and spit it into his face.

"You're not a god. You don't get to make those decisions."

"Don't I? Let's see what happens with you, shall we?"

Lord West nods toward one of the other two men in the room, and the man holds out a machine to him. I instantly recognize it as one of those TENS machines, which are used to relax taut muscles. I'm pretty certain that whatever Lord West intends to use it for, it won't be for that. He places it down next to me on the bed and presses a few buttons, and the machine fires to life.

"This was an expensive purchase for me. It may look harmless and seem like you're about to get a nice work out, but it's got a bite to it."

My skin is still wet from where the bucket of water was thrown over it. Water and electrical current don't mix, as I find out to my cost when he puts the charged, pointed prong onto the skin of my stomach. It sizzles and crackles as excruciating pain jolts through my body. I bite down so hard on my lip, willing myself not to scream, that there's the metallic taste of blood on my tongue.

Lord West laughs.

"I don't smell burning. Obviously not high enough."

He turns a dial, and I clench my stomach muscles hard, preparing for another shock. But this time the tip is placed on my left nipple, and I'm unable to stifle my scream of torment. Sharp, shooting pains burn through my body, and the stench of singed flesh enters my nostrils. I close my eyes not wanting to see what he's done to my breast.

"That's better. So much nicer to hear a scream than misplaced defiance."

"Fuck you!" I scream, and he immediately reapplies the electrical current to my inflamed nipple. "Fuck you!" I scream again through a pain so intense my head is spinning, and I'm on the verge of passing out.

"You know, they used this torture in England around the time the society was first formed. They passed some act a while later, though, which called it inhumane. If you ask me, I think it's one of my favorites, and they need to use it on some of the low-life criminals out there."

"On rapists and murderers like yourself? Why don't you let me throw a bucket of water over your minuscule dick and then see if I can find anything to stick the prong onto. Actually, scrap that. Why don't I just stick it up your fucking ass?"

The two men watching what Lord West is doing take in a sharp breath, shocked at my outburst. The devil himself, though, laughs a malevolent chuckle, which fills the room and has me shutting my eyes and imagining him tied to the bed, writhing in pain.

I hear him flick a switch on the machine, and I brace every part of my body for what's coming next. I'm panting, and my eyes flicker open just in time to see him push the electrical prong between my legs. He runs it over the outer edge of my pussy lips, and I want to cry. I'm screaming so hard my throat feels like it's ripping apart, but I won't let him break me. I can't. I need to stay whole for when William comes, and then we can end this nightmare together.

"So pretty. So very pretty."

He places the prong down and switches the machine off. I desperately try to shut my legs when I feel his tongue trace a line over the burn he's just inflicted.

"There's nothing better than a dry pussy, waiting to be ripped and torn until it's beyond repair.

He licks me again, and I can feel despair starting to take over. I need this to end.

One of the two men in the shadows steps forward. I notice he has a pair of hair cutting scissors in his hands.

"May I, My Lord?" he asks and grabs the ends of my hair, which are tied together in a pony tail.

"Of course."

The snip ricochets through my body as he severs years and years of growth from my head. I'm not sure what's causing me the most pain, at the moment – the singed flesh of my nipple and pussy, or the loss of my hair.

"My associate likes to keep hair. He's got a pretty good collection now. I don't ask what he does with it. It's not my kink."

"No. Yours is just pain and humiliation."

"Finally, she realizes. Does this hurt?"

Lord West wraps his mouth around my nipple and bites down into the scorched flesh with his teeth. I can't stand the pain. My head swims – I know I'm being dragged into unconsciousness again, and I welcome the respite from the pain. It doesn't come, though, as another bucket of icy water is thrown over me, reviving me and returning me to a world of torment. Lord West takes his three fingers again and pushes them inside me. He scissors them, and I feel my flesh tearing. He nods his head toward the other man in the room while the one from before is now standing in the corner, sniffing my freshly severed hair.

"I don't think my fingers are big enough. Let's have something else to use."

The man turns to a wooden chest in the room and pulls out one of the drawers. Retrieving a massive phallic staff, he holds it up while I'm mentally trying to squeeze my legs together as tightly as possible. William has the biggest fucking dick I've ever seen, I'm talking hung like an elephant, but that thing is like twice the size.

"This one?"

"No. The pear." Lord West's lip curls up in a smile, which has me seriously questioning his sanity for about the hundredth time.

The man by the chest roots around in the drawers and eventually brings out a metallic object. It's shaped like a pear with a device at the bottom.

"Do you know what this is?"

Lord West waves it in front of my face. I turn away, refusing to give him an answer but also knowing where the device is going, and I don't want to think about what it does.

"In Tudor times, it was a way of getting answers from criminals. It went up the ass, and then they'd gradually turn the screw." The guard who'd been standing by the chest of drawers comes over and placing his hands on either side of my neck, he jerks my head around, so I have no choice other than to face Lord West. I shut my eyes, but he forces them open with his dirty fingers. Lord West is turning the handle on the device, and I can see it opening wider and wider. The part of me concerned with self-preservation wants to start pleading with him, now, and beg him to fuck me and get it over with. However, the angry part is still in control, and it spits at him, again. A hand whacks me across my face, closely followed by a twist of my damaged nipple by the guard who cut my hair. I scream so loudly I'm sure the very foundations of the building are rattling.

Lord West winds the pear device in so it's small again and without ceremony or preparation inserts it deeply into me. It's agony, especially when he instantly turns the screw, and it begins to widen. I bare down to try and expel it from my body, but it's no use. All three men step back, and I watch as they take their dicks out and start stroking their already hardened shafts.

"It's time to take the edge off. Decorate this beautiful body with our cum, and then the real fun can start."

The two guards furiously pump their dicks while Lord West takes it slower. He switches the electrical current machine back on, and with one hand stroking himself, he uses his other hand to dot the prong all over my body. One guard cums over my face, and the other on my sore breast. Lord West is the last to find his release, which he does over my previously broken ribs. He groans out a long breath as spurt after spurt of his disgusting essence covers my skin. His lip twists again, and he brings the prong down to rub it through the sticky fluid directly over where my ribs are broken and twisted inside me. I try to stay conscious to defy the weakness in me he wants to expose, but it's too much, and the darkness claims me once again.

CHAPTER TWENTY-FIVE

WILLIAM

"When was the last time you drove?" I ask my brother who, despite being in a Lamborghini, is driving like an old grandad.

"William, I'm doing over a hundred miles an hour. If I go any faster, we'll attract the police, get pulled over, and we won't be able to get to her in time. Calm down."

"It feels slower," I protest and check the gun attached to my body for the millionth time since we got in the car.

The phone rings. I look down at the caller ID on the screen and it reads, 'Matthew Carter'. I know he's my brother's contact in all matters requiring a bit of additional help. He's ex-MI5 and still has connections there. He's also the current bodyguard for one of the richest men in the UK, a property tycoon named James North.

"Matthew?" Nicholas answers.

"Yes. We've identified the last known location of Miss Bennett's phone prior to it being, unceremoniously, returned to your house...my men are on the way there now."

"Our ETA is five minutes." Nicholas tells him.

"You'll probably be there before my men. You going in alone?"

"Yes," I reply before giving my brother a chance to say no. I'm not going to leave Tamara alone with Lord West for a minute longer than I have to. I know exactly what the bastard is capable of, and I refuse to let Tamara be subjected to that while I wait around outside for reinforcements.

The line remains silent while my brother neither confirms nor denies what we are going to do when we get to our location.

"I understand. I'd do the same for my woman," Matthew finally responds. "Do whatever you need to, to get her out safely. My men can handle the aftermath."

"Thank you," Nicholas replies. "So, what do I owe James this time?"

Matthew laughs down his end of the phone.

"I think he'd like to surprise his wife with a title of some sort for Christmas. Perhaps you could have a word in Prince John's ear. I know you and he have been close in the past."

"If you're suggesting I've fucked alongside him, then yes I have, but not since Victoria came into my life."

"He's too busy being ridden cowboy style by his pregnancy hormone flooded wife," I mutter without thinking. Damn. That's one of those filter things I'm supposed to remember.

There is too much etiquette when it comes to society. Why can't we just say what we want and not have to mind our tongues.

"Good to hear it." Matthew chuckles at my faux pas.

"I'll see what I can do," Nicholas answers.

"Be careful. Call me when it's over."

"Will do." My brother ends the call, and we pull over in a densely forested area. Up ahead, I can see an opening, which appears to lead to a long driveway. There are one or two other houses scattered around but nothing that would cause major issues if we make a bit of a disturbance.

We're dressed all in black – our standard uniform for returning artwork seems to have transformed into the perfect outfit for rescuing damsels in distress and slaying the bad guys without a spot of blood showing.

It's dark out, the winter sun having set hours ago. Nicholas pulls down his night vision goggles, and I do the same.

"We go in the back way. You got your silencer?"

"Yes," I reply.

"Stay together. Follow my orders. We'll get her out."

"I know. You've got my word...no heroics. You've got a wife and baby to go back to, and I've got a woman to repair." I reply, reassuring my brother that I'm not going to go all commando on him and lose my head in there.

"She's stronger than you think. She'll give Lord West a run for his money."

"I hope so."

We go silent and switch on the intercoms in our ears. Like lions creeping slowly up on their prey, we make strides through the trees toward our target – a dimly lit house in front of us. It's old and a little run down. The perfect ghost house for Lord West's activities. I shudder as I think about the number of girls whose last view of the outside world was this building.

"Guard at eleven o'clock." Nicholas' voice comes through the intercom in my ear.

"Got him."

"Take him," my brother orders.

The guard is around the side of the building, having a crafty cigarette. He can't be seen by the other guards on lookout. I pull my knife from its holder on my trousers, and before he has a chance to notice, I'm next to him and have sliced through his throat.

"Shouldn't smoke. It's bad for your health in more ways than one," I tell him as he falls to the ground dead.

Dragging him, I deposit the body out of sight. Nicholas and I then press our bodies closely to the wall and shuffle around the building toward an entrance we'd examined earlier on Google maps. What a wonderful invention, but there's no privacy in the world any longer.

My feet shuffle, and I hit something heavy. I stop abruptly, and Nicholas knocks into the back of me. Looking down, I realize it's another body.

"What is it?" Nicholas asks.

"A body?" Not quite understanding. There's little light in the area, but through my goggles, I can make out a gunshot wound in his head.

"What?"

"Looks like a guard." I examine his clothing and see a knife attached to his trousers.

"Did you kill him?" Nicholas asks.

"No. You saw me deposit the guy I killed in the bushes over there."

"Someone must have pissed West off. Pretty messy clean up if you ask me."

"Maybe he's busy and will sort it out later?" The second the words leave my mouth, they turn my stomach because I don't want to think what he's doing to Tamara in the house. "Let's worry about it later. I want to get inside."

"Keep leading," Nicholas orders, and we peer around the side of the building.

"I've got two talking," I tell Nicholas.

He peaks over my shoulder.

"Confirmed."

"Shoot, or try to take them out in person?"

"Person. It's quieter and less chance of missing."

"Agreed."

On my count," Nicholas starts. "Three…two…"

"Fuck." I exclaim as a bright light illuminates the garden area, and our hiding place is discovered. We both rip off the night vision glasses and bring our guns up ready to shoot. It's no use, though, as I can't see a thing.

"Your Grace, Earl Lullington." A man steps forward, and I get ready to fire, but we're both quickly captured, and our weapons along with our earpieces are removed.

"If you'd follow me." The man indicates the path we are to take. I have a guard behind me and two on either side – Nicholas has the same. I'm not restrained, and I look to my brother for orders. His face is a mix of deep thought and concern. With a nod of his head, he signals we are to see where we are led, for now. I don't doubt it will be to see West, and where West is Tamara will be, so I'll happily oblige, for now.

I'm mentally bracing myself for the state I'll find Tamara in.

I wear my emotions with no filter, but I can't show them to her. She'll need the strength the monster inside me imparts when I first see her. I can't show weakness. We enter through a small door into what I suspect is the lounge. The building is incredibly run down – the ornate paintings and wall hangings are littered with spider webs, and there is enough dust covering the gothic sculptures on antique wooden furniture to write my name in. This place hasn't been inhabited in years. It's unloved – a place where the terrors are real. I control my emotions with a deep breath while we wait for the door to open. What I don't expect on the other side is Lord West on his hands and knees with two guards on either side of him. He has a gun pointed at his head, and two men lie already executed on the floor in the corner of the room with blood pooling around them. Tamara sits on a sofa wrapped in a blanket. There are newly forming bruises on her face, which is wet with a mixture of fresh tears and blood. Her beautiful, long hair has been cut short.

"William." She tries to get to her feet when she sees me, but her legs are wobbly, and she sinks back down. I look to the man who led us here. He motions for me to go to her. I do so and wrap my arms around her.

"What happened? Are you hurt?"

"There will be time for questions later, Earl Lullington. Our business here is concluded, now," the man speaks and steps forward with a note for my brother. He also hands my brother back his gun. "I suspect you have reinforcements on the way. I'll allow them to do the clean-up operation." The man whistles, and everyone leaves the room. Lord West suddenly realizes he's free and scrambles to get to his feet. Nicholas is quicker, though, and points the gun at him.

"Back down."

Lord West's eyes are filled with menace, and my brother's

are laced with confusion but also determination. Lord West understands this and gets back down onto his knees in the center of the room.

"I think I want to see what's going on here."

My brother keeps his eyes and gun trained on West but comes over to me. He drops the note into my hands.

"If you would, Brother."

I open it and read it aloud.

"I'm afraid I couldn't wait for you to play heroes this time. There will be other opportunities, though. This isn't over yet. Take care of my daughters, both of them. They are not Lord West's to destroy. Viscount Hamilton."

"Viscount Hamilton," Nicholas repeats. "They were his men?"

Lord West snorts.

"Seems the old man got one up on you."

Nicholas strides forward and uses the barrel of the gun to smack him over the head. I turn my attention back to Tamara.

"What did he do to you? Apart from this." I stroke her tufted hair.

She lowers the sheet a little to bare her breast. It's inflamed and blackened. The skin burned on the tip.

"Lower?"

"Yes," she whimpers. I shut my eyes, trying to keep hold of my control. "Let the monster out," she pleads with me. My eyes flash open, and she turns her head toward the corner of the room. In the shadows under a table, I can just about make out a figure.

"He had her here. One of the missing girls."

"Joanna?" Nicholas asks.

"No," Tamara replies. "The one you believed your father killed, Daphne Knight."

"Shit!" Nicholas exclaims. "You're a sick fuck." He whacks West again, and the man slumps to the floor. Nicholas stomps over toward the girl and whimpered pleas can be heard coming from the shadows. They turn into song, and it sends shivers down my spine. Nicholas grabs a lamp from a nearby table and points it down, so he can see the girl. What we find there is not the Daphne Knight I saw sold that day at the auction. She's lost an eye, and the socket is infected and inflamed. Her hair is shaved short. She has scars, cuts, and bruises all over her body, and several of her fingers are missing. Her leg is at an odd angle, obviously, having been broken at some point and not allowed to heal properly.

"No, no, no, no," she sings. It's obvious that the young girl she once was has completely gone. I know in my heart there's no hope for her.

"Daphne." Nicholas motions for her to come to him. She shakes her head.

"I won't hurt you."

"It hurts already."

"I know it does." He keeps his voice even and low. I pull Tamara close to my chest. She doesn't need to see this.

"He said it would stop one day, and the angels would come and take me to heaven. Just like the baby he beat from me. Just like the parts of my body he took already. He won't kill me, though. He said that would be too easy. I'm one of the special girls. I can withstand anything for the society, but I don't want to anymore. I want to sleep, but I've forgotten how."

I can see how visibly shaken my brother is. He's always blamed himself for these girls. They were given to him, and Daphne was one of the one's he didn't choose.

"Come to me, Daphne. The angels are here. I can see them.

Tamara starts to squirm in my arms. She realizes what Nicholas is about to do.

"He can't," she whimpers into my chest.

"It's the only way. That's not a human anymore. It's no life. Trust me, I know."

I don't look as the gun goes off behind us, but I know Daphne has finally found her peace. Tamara lets out a cry of loss.

"Do you want this, Brother?" Nicholas asks, indicating toward Lord West who remains semi-conscious on the floor.

"No. Just end him. I want to take Tamara home."

Nicholas strides purposefully over to West and kicks him until he starts to stir. He doesn't give him any last words, or prayers for redemption in heaven or hell. No, he fires the gun twice. The first shot destroys that piece of his anatomy he was so proud of. The second is straight between his eyes and ends his pitiful existence.

CHAPTER TWENTY-SIX

TAMARA

*T*hree months later

"Why do those people have to queue when we get to walk straight through and onto the plane?" William asks me as he flashes his ticket toward the flight attendant.

"We're in first-class," I tell him and show the lady my ticket.

"Thank you, ma'am." The attendant gives me a little smirk, and we walk down the corridor toward the plane.

"It's not because you told them I have autism?"

"No. We've paid to board first."

"But if I didn't want to pay, could we tell them?"

"Yes, we could," I reply and wrap my hand around his.

"Then it does work the same way as it did at that theme park we went to, and you told them about me, so I didn't have to queue."

"It does, but you've got money, and I don't plan on flying economy when you can afford a first-class flight."

"Ok."

William strides confidently toward the next waiting attendant at the entrance to the plane.

"Welcome, sir." The lady bows her head to him. I show her our tickets. "You're seats one and two to the left. I believe you are the only people in first-class for the flight. You'll have a dedicated attendant. If you need anything, please just ask."

"Thank you."

William starts to stride off to our seats but then pauses, and I can only just suppress the laugh threatening to escape because I know what's coming next.

"How many years of flight practice has the captain had?"

"I'm sorry, sir?" the lady at the door responds.

"Flight hours?"

"A lot. He's one of the most decorated in the company."

She gives him her well-worn smile.

"And the co-pilot?" William continues, standing there next to me.

"I believe roughly two thousand. Miss Lewis is a fantastic pilot, as well."

"A woman?" William questions, and I know it's not a sexist remark. It's because all the information he's been frantically researching on the journey to Heathrow airport has been related to male pilots. "Do they have the same training?"

"Yes, sir."

The footsteps of the other passengers start to echo down the corridor as they approach.

"Right. It didn't say anything about that?"

"What didn't, sir?"

"Female pilots. The internet."

The attendant looks at me and I mouth, 'first time'. She nods with understanding.

"I can assure you women pilots are as safe as men. It's proven."

"But I didn't read that."

The other passengers arrive, and the attendant tries to turn away to greet them.

"One more thing."

"Yes, sir."

"The fuel. Has the pilot used the standard calculation for it? We need to make sure we've got enough to get to the Caribbean."

The eyes of a little boy waiting with the other passengers go wide, and he tugs on his mother's jacket with worry.

"I can assure you the pilot has had all her calculations checked, and the plane is full enough."

"Good, I know it's seventy thousand kilograms of fuel to get to New York, so she'll need more than that."

"William"–I tap his arm– "can we go start our honeymoon, now, please?"

He looks between me and the flight attendant.

"Of course. Thank you."

To a relieved exhale from both the flight staff and the passengers, my new husband finally decides to take his seat.

"You're suddenly very bossy," he tells me.

"You can talk!" I roll my eyes at him and put my bag down

to pull out my Kindle for the flight. "Wasn't it little more than seven hours ago you picked me up out of bed, threw me over your shoulder, and carried me to the family church where you demanded—in front of Victoria, Nicholas, and a vicar—that we marry then and there."

"You didn't like my proposal?"

I laugh at him and pop my new Marc Jacobs bag into the overhead locker.

"It was a little unorthodox. Put it that way."

"I thought there was less chance of you saying no, doing it like that."

"That's true." I slide into the seat next to him.

"Are you happy?"

"To be Lady William Cavendish?"

"Yes." He turns to me with a look of worry in his eyes.

"I couldn't be happier."

"Good, because we're going to spend the next two weeks putting a baby in your belly."

I roll my eyes at him.

"You're not joking, are you?"

He shrugs his shoulders and then does his seat belt up.

"When have you known me to joke?"

"Never. It's one of the things I like about you along with the fact you find it impossible to lie."

"What else do you like about me?" he asks while he pulls a thick blanket out and places it over my lap. I'm wearing a summer dress, having left my thick coat with Nicholas and Victoria when they dropped us at the airport. Victoria was moaning she was the size of a house and wished she could go to the Caribbean. Nicholas promised it would be the first place they would go to as soon as the baby was old enough to be left with Auntie Tamara and Uncle William. William and I laughed at that because we both know Nicholas would never let his child out of his sight for more than a few minutes. Victoria and I have bodyguards with us constantly. The threats may have died down, for now, but Viscount Hamilton is out there somewhere, and there's also another missing girl still to be found.

"Do you think Joanna's still alive?" I change the conversation abruptly.

William sucks air into his mouth.

"After this much time, I doubt it. If she is, you saw the condition Daphne was in. I guess we have to hope that somewhere, deep down, Viscount Hamilton does have a heart. He saved you from West before I could, and I'll owe him forever for that. It took you long enough to heal from the injuries West inflicted on you, and he only had you for a short time."

I shift in my seat still thinking of the pain of that day, and the scarring to my left nipple. It will never heal properly, and it's unlikely I'll be able to use it to feed my babies (How many had William threatened to have with me?). But I'll deal with that when the time comes. My ribs still give me a bit of pain, but that's to be expected in England with the damp weather even in the summer. The main thing is Lord West didn't break me. William and I still have the same sex life we did before I was taken. We both have a passion for the darker side of things, and I trust William with how far he'll go.

Before we left Lord West's property to burn down, that night, I'll always remember his words as he removed the dead deviant's brain from his skull and threw it on the fire. *'People say my brain is wired wrong, but I think his was. Woman are not creatures to be destroyed. They are to be worshiped and loved. Treated with kindness and devotion. Lord West was the wrong one. Not me.'*

When all this is finally over, whether we are alive or dead, that will be William's epitaph forever because he's not wrong. He's unique, my husband, and I love him.

"I love you too," he whispers into my ear.

"Did I say that out loud?"

"No, I can just read the goofy look on your face."

"I did not have a goofy look."

"Oh, you did. It was something like this."

He pulls a funny face, and I can't help but pull him into a kiss.

"Do you think the monster wants to come out and play for a bit?"

"On the plane?" He raises an eyebrow.

"Maybe only a little bit of the monster until we reach our destination."

He licks his lips, and we both sit back in our seats. William slides his hand under my blanket as the plane starts to taxi down the runway. As we thunder into the air twisting and turning until we're level, he brings me to an orgasm with three of his fingers inside me. Reminding me just who owns my pussy.

EPILOGUE

JOANNA

"*Is* anyone there?" I sit up in my bed when I hear the bang of a heavy door in the darkness I've become so accustomed to. "Hello?" I shout again, but there's no answer. It's my mind playing tricks on me, again. It often does that. The worst times are when it imagines I'm no longer in this place. That I've been whisked away to a different life, in a different country with a new identity, and I'm a new person living somewhere where the Oakfield Society doesn't exist. A place where I can make decisions for myself. One where he doesn't come in the night and abuse me because he can't have *her*.

The door opens, and I jump from my bed to stand beside it as I've been taught. My hands clenched behind my back, my head bowed, and my legs slightly parted in the ill-fitting nightdress I wear. I don't look up. No, that would be wrong. I did once, and I couldn't get out of bed for a week because the bruising was so bad. I must wait...wait for him...my father.

"Good evening, Joanna," Viscount Hamilton addresses me.

"Good evening, Daddy," I reply in the only manner I know, now.

"I have a present for you."

"Thank you," I reply, still not raising my head. I've not been told I can, yet.

"I'll give it to you soon. I need to vent my anger first."

He shifts a chair and takes a seat in it. I stand painfully still. My leg muscles are weak, and my eyes are unable to adjust easily to the light in the room. I wonder how long I've been here? It feels like an eternity. It could be weeks, months or years – everything has blurred into one. Day and night merged into a perpetual darkness.

The door opens and closes again. I know it's Camilla, the lady who looks after me.

"Your drink." I hear her place the glass down on a table.

"Thank you," the Viscount replies. "Joanna. Come sit on my lap."

I do as I'm ordered. I don't even question it anymore.

"I hope she behaves for you tonight," Camilla tells the Viscount, but I know that's a warning for me. She doesn't need to worry, though. Her training has all been received and understood. I'm the perfect woman, now, and I'm ready for my future.

Camilla leaves, and I take my place on the Viscount's lap.

He instantly bunches my skirt up and rubs his hand over my pussy. I used to protest and scream when he did this. I'd curse him and try to escape, but I'm so broken, now, I don't even flinch when he sticks a finger inside me.

"My daughter had her baby, today? A girl, which I knew it would be. It's fitting that Oakfield finally has a female. All we need now is for you to marry Theodore and conceive a male, and our family can rule again."

He pushes another finger in, and my body tightens with the need to expel him.

"That's not behaving like the good wife I've taught you to be. He won't want that."

"Please." I let the little whimper fall from my lips with regret.

"Too late." He withdraws his hand and pushes me to the floor. "Tonight, will have to be our last time. I can't take any more risks with you. On the bed. Clothes off, and legs apart."

I know what comes next: the degradation, the pain, and the feelings of disgust. There is still a tiny part of me that wants to protest and tell him to go fuck himself in the ass with a sharp knife. Inform him I'm never opening my legs for him again. But I don't. I get to my feet. I strip out of my nightgown, and I lie back on the bed and part my legs to give him a view of what he will abuse shortly.

Viscount Hamilton removes his clothes. He's not a handsome man. His physique is aged and not well looked after. He strides to the bed, and I try to will my body to relax because it hurts less that way. It refuses to listen, though, knowing too well the suffering it's preparing for. He leans down over me then pops up again. I hope for a moment he's changed his mind.

"I almost forgot. Your present." He reaches for a box he must have placed on the table when he entered the room. He opens the lid and pulls out a black wig. "This is your special present to me."

He comes to the side of the bed and rearranges the wig over my hair. The hair is long and styled just like *hers* is in all the pictures he's shown me of her.

"Perfect." He stands back. "And to think the man who took it from her head thought he would get to keep it. My men soon destroyed those illusions when they put a bullet in his brain."

The Viscount strokes himself a few times.

"First it's time to see whether Tamara lives up to her mother's standards. Then it's time for you to get married and for me to become the ruler of Oakfield. With you married to my son, I'll be able to manipulate him into working against the Cavendish brothers and my daughters. They will all be destroyed, and a new leader will be chosen for the society, and I'm next in line."

THE END

The Dark Sovereignty Series continues with
A FATHER'S INSISTENCE

Coming March 2019

Joanna and Theo's story.

AFTERWORD

William's autism is not the cause of his darkness, however, throughout the book he's worried it is. He needs Tamara to show him he's been tainted by his father's treatment of him. For anyone to be locked away in a room alone for most of their life would leave them with issues, not only that but also William's father introduced him to sex, and his version of what it should be – abusive in the Duke's case. William has seen murder, he's seen violence, and it's all he's been taught until he meets Tamara and discovers a love different from the affection he holds for his brother, Nicholas. What he and Tamara engage in is consensual, and they are hopelessly devoted to each other. William and his brother are striving to rid the world of the evil of the Oakfield Society. They are the good guys, just having to do bad things to make everything right.

Autism DOES NOT make William a monster. He's a hot, alpha male with a taste for the dark side. My kind of guy!

Thank you for reading.

Anna xx

COMING SOON

A FATHER'S INSISTENCE

Coming March 2019.
Joanna and Theodore's story.

One of five women who endured horrific trials to win the hand of Nicholas Cavendish, Lady Joanna Nethercutt suffered greatly throughout the ordeal, ultimately losing to Victoria Hamilton. She swiftly finds herself sold by her own father, who's determined she'll be of use to him yet. For a year, she's "trained" in preparation for marriage to Victoria's brother, with whom she'll be expected to produce heirs that will one day strengthen and continue the very society responsible for all of Joanna's torment.

In the space of a breath, Theodore Hamilton is thrust into a secret society he knew nothing about, and married to a woman who seems terrified of his very existence. Suddenly, his carefree yet honorable life is filled with secrets and shadows, allies and enemies, leaving Theodore unsure who to trust...starting with his broken bride. His lure to the delicate beauty is tempered by external influence, lies and manipulation from all sides.

In this breathless conclusion to the Dark Sovereignty series, Theodore must decide where his loyalties lie, and race to destroy the evil men responsible for the immeasurable suffering of everyone he holds dear—including the wife he never wanted, but can't possibly live without.

And don't forget.....

Legacy of Succession, Dark Sovereignty, Book 1:

Let's build a better world together
rather than just extinguish the fires of hate.
~ Dark Sovereignty Series by Anna Edwards

ACKNOWLEDGMENTS

First and always to my great friend, Charity Hendry, for always being there for me. For entertaining my crazy ideas and helping me bring them to fruition. Love you to bits.

To my editor, Tracy Roelle, and proofreader, Sheena Taylor, you polish my books so that they shine brightly. I'm lucky to have such a good team.

To my street team, thank you so much for all you that you do to get my books out in the reader world.

To Yvonne, for not only beta reading and offering me advice but for organizing so much when it comes to conventions. I'd be lost without you.

To my family, thank you for all the support that you give me.

Finally, to all the readers who have embraced me as an author.

I'm so glad that you enjoy the stories my mind creates. I hope I'm able to give you many more years of pleasure.

THE CONTROL SERIES

The Control Series: A dramatic, witty, and sensual suspense romance set predominantly in London.

Surrendered Control, The Control Series, Book 1:

Divided Control, The Control Series, Book 2:

Misguided Control, The Control Series, Book 3:

Controlling Darkness, The Control Series, Book 4:

Controlling Heritage, The Control Series, Book 5:

Controlling Disgrace, The Control Series, Book 6:

Controlling the Past, The Control Series, Book 7:

THE GLACIAL BLOOD

The Touch of Snow, The Glacial Blood Series, Book 1

Fighting the Lies, The Glacial Blood Series, Book 2:

Fallen for Shame, The Glacial Blood Series, Book 3:

Shattered Fears, The Glacial Blood Series, Book 4:

Coming Soon to the Glacial Blood Series...
Hidden Pain – Hunter, Lily and Kingsley's story
Stolen Choices – Katia's story
Power of a Myth – Molly and Hayden's story
A Deadly Affair – Jessica's story
Banishing Regrets – Kas' story.

ABOUT THE AUTHOR

I am a British author, from the depths of the rural countryside near London. In a previous life, I was an accountant from the age of twenty-one. I still do that on occasions, but most of my life is now spent intermingling writing while looking after my husband, two children and two cats (probably in the inverse order to the one listed!). When I have some spare time, I can also be found writing poetry, baking cakes (and eating them), or behind a camera snapping like a mad paparazzo.

I'm an avid reader who turned to writing to combat my depression and anxiety. I have a love of traveling and like to bring this to my stories to give them the air of reality.

I like my heroes hot and hunky with a dirty mouth, my heroines demure but with spunk, and my books full of dramatic suspense.

CONNECT WITH ANNA EDWARDS
www.AuthorAnnaEdwards.com
Email: anna1000edwards@gmail.com

MEET THE AUTHOR

I'll be at the following signings:

21-24 February - Wild Wicked Weekend, San Antonio, Texas, USA
2nd March – Leeds Author Event, Leeds, UK
1st June – Heart of Steel, Sheffield, UK.
18-19 October – Shameless, Orlando, Florida, US

Printed in Poland
by Amazon Fulfillment
Poland Sp. z o.o., Wrocław